How to Write a Bestselling Paranormal Romance

Vamp Up Your Novel with Supernatural Sizzle

Just Bae

Contents

Introduction

Welcome to the enchanting world of paranormal romance, where love and the supernatural intertwine to create captivating stories that transport readers to realms beyond their wildest dreams. As an aspiring writer of this genre, it's essential to understand what sets paranormal romance apart and what key elements you need to include to craft a compelling narrative. In this chapter, we will explore the definition of paranormal romance, its key elements, and how it differs from other romance genres.

Paranormal romance is a subgenre of romance that incorporates elements of the supernatural, fantastical, or otherworldly into the love story. This can include anything from vampires, werewolves, ghosts, and witches to more obscure beings like fairies, demons, and shapeshifters. The core of a paranormal romance is still the romantic relationship between the protagonists, but it is set against a backdrop that includes supernatural occurrences and beings. This blend of romance and the paranormal creates a unique and thrilling reading experience that captivates fans of both romance and fantasy.

One of the key elements of paranormal romance is the presence of supernatural beings or phenomena. These elements add an extra layer of excitement and intrigue to the story. For example, a love story between a human and a vampire can explore themes of immortality, forbidden love, and the struggle between human and supernatural worlds. The paranormal aspects should be well-integrated into the plot, enhancing the romance rather than overshadowing it. The supernatural elements should feel natural and believable within the context of the story's world.

Another essential element is the setting. Paranormal romances often take place in richly imagined worlds that blend the familiar with the fantastical. This could be a modern city where supernatural beings live hidden among humans, a historical setting with a twist of magic, or an entirely fictional realm where anything is possible. The setting should be vividly described and consistent, providing a backdrop that enhances the story's mood and themes. World-building is crucial in paranormal romance, as it helps readers suspend disbelief and become fully immersed in the story.

Character development is also vital in paranormal romance. The protagonists should be well-rounded and relatable, even if they possess supernatural abilities. Their motivations, desires, and conflicts should be clear and compelling. The romantic relationship should be at the heart of the story, with the characters' personal growth and development intertwined with their romantic journey. The supernatural elements should serve to heighten the stakes and add depth to the characters' interactions and conflicts.

Paranormal romance differs from other romance genres primarily in its incorporation of supernatural elements. While contemporary romance focuses on realistic, everyday love stories, and historical romance is set in specific historical periods, paranormal romance breaks the boundaries of reality. It allows for more creative freedom and exploration of themes that wouldn't be possible in a purely realistic setting. This genre often includes high-stakes conflicts, such as battles between good and evil or the struggle to protect loved ones from supernatural threats, adding an extra layer of excitement and tension.

In contrast to fantasy romance, which also includes fantastical elements, paranormal romance typically takes place in a world that is recognizable to readers, with the supernatural elements hidden or integrated into everyday life. Fantasy romance often involves entirely fictional worlds with their own rules and histories, whereas paranormal romance blends the familiar with the extraordinary. This makes paranormal romance more accessible to readers who enjoy stories set in the real world but with a twist of magic or the supernatural.

The themes explored in paranormal romance can also set it apart from other genres. Common themes include the clash between the human and supernatural worlds, the exploration of immortality and its impact on relationships, and the idea of forbidden love. These themes add depth and complexity to the romance, allowing for rich story-telling and emotional resonance. The supernatural elements can serve as metaphors for real-life issues, such as identity, acceptance, and overcoming prejudice, making the stories both entertaining and thought-provoking.

Writing paranormal romance requires a delicate balance between the romantic and supernatural elements. The romance should always be at the forefront, with the super-natural aspects enhancing the story rather than detracting from it. It's important to create a believable and consistent world where the supernatural elements feel natural and integral to the plot. This involves careful world-building, well-developed characters, and a strong, engaging storyline that keeps readers invested in both the romance and the paranormal aspects.

As you embark on your journey to write a paranormal romance, remember to draw inspiration from the rich history and mythology of the supernatural. Research different myths, legends, and folklore to add depth and authenticity to your story. Consider how the supernatural elements can serve as metaphors for real-life issues and enhance the emotional impact of the romance. The more thought and creativity you put into your world-building and character development, the more compelling your story will be.

Paranormal romance is a unique and exciting genre that combines the thrill of the supernatural with the emotional depth of a love story. By understanding its key elements and how it differs from other romance genres, you can craft a captivating narrative that will enchant and engage your readers. Focus on creating a believable and immersive world, developing well-rounded characters, and weaving together the romantic and supernatural elements in a way that enhances both. With these tools and insights, you're well on your way to writing a bestselling paranormal romance.

Chapter 1

Popular Paranormal Creatures

When writing a paranormal romance, one of the most important decisions you'll make is which supernatural beings to incorporate into your story. There are countless myths and legends to draw from across human history, but certain paranormal creatures stand out as especially popular in this genre. In this chapter, we'll explore some of the top supernatural beings used in paranormal romance and how you can effectively incorporate them into your own writing.

One of the most ubiquitous paranormal romance creatures is the vampire. Vampires bring built-in drama, intrigue, and romance to any narrative. As immortal beings, vampiric characters introduce compelling themes of everlasting love, the consequences of immortality, and the struggle between their human and monstrous natures. When writing vampire characters, you can play with variations in their abilities, like whether they can turn into bats or withstand sunlight. Just be sure to establish the "rules" of your vampires early on and maintain consistency. Describe their appearances, feeding habits, powers, weaknesses, and social structures to create richly-realized vampire worlds for readers to get lost in.

Another immensely popular paranormal creature is the werewolf. Werewolves bridge the gap between wild animal instincts and human emotion and rationality. Having your protagonist fall for a werewolf spices up the classic "taming the beast" trope. Full moons, pack dynamics, and the painful process of shapeshifting provide lots of opportunities for dramatic tension. You might establish werewolf characters who struggle to control their volatile shifts between human and wolf form. Or perhaps your werewolves proudly embrace their lupine natures as superior to feeble humankind. Make sure to describe the transformative process and its physical and emotional impacts in vivid sensory detail.

Ghosts also feature prominently in paranormal romance. The key to compelling ghost characters is anchoring them with emotional backstories and unfinished business that keeps them tethered to the mortal plane. Is your ghostly spirit a brooding Gothic hero pining for his lost love? Or a vivacious Jazz-age specter seeking one last dance? Ghosts can struggle to communicate, interact with physical objects, or be seen by living beings—creating barriers to intimacy that ratchet up romantic tension. Describe apparitions, chilling touches, mysterious voices and sounds, and possessions to terrify and tantalize your readers.

Beyond these "big three" creatures lie endless possibilities. Many paranormal romance authors incorporate mythological beings from diverse folklores, including Greek, Celtic, East Asian, Native American, and more. For instance, you might feature fairies as protagonists, borrowing from the capricious tricksters of British Isles lore or the small, insect-winged spirits of Victorian flower fairy paintings. Just take care not to trivialize or appropriate cultural traditions not your own. Witches are another popular choice, allowing you to create intricate magical systems and explore moral questions around using power responsibly. You can also tap into lesser-known legends like shapeshifters, mermaids, banshees, ghouls, incubi/succubi, and more for fresh takes on paranormal romance.

When selecting paranormal creatures, consider the themes and conflicts they will help you explore. Vampires symbolize dangerous seduction, forbidden desires, and the struggle between darkness and light. Werewolves represent animal impulses versus human rationality. Ghosts speak to undying love and unfinished business carrying on after death. Think about the metaphors that resonate most strongly with your story and choose creatures accordingly. Just remember that no matter which paranormal beings you ultimately pick, the romance itself should take center stage. Use supernatural elements to raise the stakes and advance character development rather than overshadowing the relationships at the heart of your tale.

Whichever creatures you end up featuring, thorough world-building is essential. Establish consistent supernatural "rules" regarding your paranormal beings' powers, weaknesses, origins, societies, and more. Seamlessly integrate them into settings like small towns, big cities, alternate dimensions, or entirely fictional realms. Make the extraordinary feel believable by rendering rich sensory details—the crunch of a vampire biting into a neck, the earthy musk of a werewolf's pelt, the ethereal glow enveloping a ghost. Immerse readers in worlds where the paranormal seems normal and romance can thrive alongside magic, mystery, and the supernatural.

Other popular paranormal romance character options like vampires, werewolves, and ghosts have compelling built-in metaphors and intriguing abilities that spice up romantic plots. However, readers often crave fresh takes on the supernatural. That's where tapping into more obscure myths and legends can inspire creativity. One approach is featuring fairies, witches, or other magical beings from humanity's rich lore.

Fairies stem from ancient European folklore and encompass a wide variety of magical spirits, including clever tricksters, imperious nobles, kindly helpers, and sinister villains. Common fairy traits involve close ties to nature, secretive societies hidden just out of human sight, capriciousness toward mortals, and beguiling beauty. In your writing, establishing unique fairy social structures, magical systems, physical descriptions, and emotional temperaments can yield multi-dimensional fairy characters. Play with variations like seasonal court affiliations, tiny insect-like vs. human-sized bodies, or different bases of fairy power—herbalism, illusion, prophesy, etc.

You also have unlimited choices for crafting witch characters whose magical practices form the core of your paranormal worlds. From benevolent healers to dark crones, modern Wiccans to traditional spell-casters, your witches can abide by moral codes or pursue their own agendas—making them complex protagonists and antagonists whose powers move the plot. Build coherent magical systems with defined scope and costs rather than generic "hocus pocus." Outline spellcasting rituals, potion brewing processes, familiars, covens, herb-lore, astrology ties, and other details for realistic worldbuilding.

Reaching even further back in human history, mythological beings intertwine with ancient belief systems but remain shrouded in mystery. Goddesses, demigods, muses, satyrs, nymphs, and other elusive figures offer new takes on paranormal romance. Just take care to avoid appropriating sensitive religious and cultural traditions not your own. Creatures from Native American skin-walkers to Hindu nagas to Japanese yokai possess rich narrative potential if handled respectfully.

No matter which lesser-known paranormal creatures you feature, the key is blending romance and magic in innovative ways. Have witches charm irresistible potions to find true love or fairy monarchs forbid trysts with humans. Perhaps mythological beings lose immortality when they fall for mortals against divine law. Just ensure the supernatural drives character growth and relationships rather than overshadowing them.

Ultimately, any being from fantasy, myth, or legend can be molded into original paranormal romance characters. So tap into humankind's collective lore for inspiration when vampires and werewolves grow tiresome. With so many stories still untold, fairies, witches, and obscure mythological creatures offer exciting new means to infuse age-old themes of love and transformation with fresh supernatural twists.

Chapter 2

More on Vampires, Werewolves and Ghost

Vampires, werewolves, and ghosts have long been staples in the paranormal romance genre. These creatures of the dark are often portrayed as mysterious, powerful and dangerous, which heightens the thrilling element of the narratives. Their eerie and appealing aura often veils a depth of emotion that can occasionally surpass that of their human companions. The use of these supernatural creatures in romance literature allows authors to explore complex themes of love, desire, morality, and the human condition. The immortal character of vampires, for instance, means an eternal love that can inspire or decimate depending on the path the story takes.

From the enigmatic characters in Stephenie Meyer's Twilight series to the tormented heroes in J.R. Ward's *Black Dagger Brotherhood*, vampires have consistently stolen the hearts of readers. Their eternal youth, combined with centuries of knowledge, provides a unique blend of youthful passion and an old-fashioned sense of romance. Furthermore, the ever-present danger that comes with loving a creature of the night adds a layer of thrill and uncertainty to their relationships. Subsequently, vampire-human relationships communicate the notion of forbidden love, embodying the axiom that the most desirable things are often the most dangerous.

Werewolves, on the other hand, bring a different energy into the world of paranormal romance. Love stories involving werewolves tend to integrate the theme of duality, reflecting the two sides of their nature – the human and the beast. In these narratives, love becomes a nexus point for the tension between the creature's primal instincts and human compassion. This experience furthers the emotional depth of the story as love is tried under these challenging circumstances and often emerges triumphant, glorifying the power of human connection.

The physicality of werewolves and their raw power is a recurring theme in these novels. Yet alongside the allure of their brute strength is an emotional vulnerability that draws readers in. The dichotomy between strong and gentle presents an expressive medium to explore the complexities of love and courtship. The vibrant and heated scenes of werewolf dynamics give way to engaging explorations of pack commitment, alpha/beta dynamics, and the importance of loyalty and trust in love and relationships.

In contrast to vampires and werewolves, ghosts carry a sense of melancholic romance. Ghost-human love stories often revolve around unresolved issues from the past, transcendent love, and sometimes, even personal redemption. Ghost characters are often bound by the realms of the living and the dead, making their narratives less about physical desire and more about emotional bonding and companionship. This imparts a transcendent and almost ethereal quality to such love stories, emphasizing love's potential to endure beyond material existence.

The presence of ghosts in paranormal romance allows for the exploration of time, memory, and the weight of past actions on present circumstances. The tragic undertone of these narratives is often the ghost's inability to physically interact with their loved ones, highlighting the profound emotions and spiritual connections that define human relationships. Ghostly love stories may offer melancholic endings with the specter's eventual departure, thereby underlining the ephemeral nature of life and love.

Nonetheless, all these protagonists embody a 'monster' with a heart, one who struggles between their dark nature and their yearning for love and acceptance. This juxtaposition of fear and affection, of horror and beauty, creates an incredible pull for readers. The seemingly insurmountable barriers echoing societal norms and prejudices enable the authors to dive deep into the essence of humanity's emotional capacity and the lengths, and depths, it can reach when put to the test.

Taken together, each archetype—vampires, werewolves, and ghosts—offers a specific perspective on the dynamics of love and relationships. Vampires, with their immortal lives and persistent youth, can explore the unfading nature of love. Werewolves show the struggles of duality and beastly nature, while ghosts emphasize love's potential to transcend the parameters of life and death.

These supernatural entities, each with their own unique traits, intensify the passion, tension, and emotional journey in their respective narratives. They allow writers to push the boundaries of traditional romance narratives and explore more complex, thrilling, and engaging love stories. Still, the heart of the narrative remains the same - the exploration of love, its complexities, struggle, pain, and eternal hope.

Even as these paranormal characters navigate their identities, their conflicts often mirror the conflicts of the reader. Their tales can be seen as a metaphor for self-discovery, acceptance, and learning to love, despite perceived flaws and differences. As such, the genre of paranormal romance, with its central figures of vampires, werewolves, and ghosts, continues to captivate readers because of its depth, resonance, and, of course, its compelling depiction of love.

In conclusion, vampires, werewolves, and ghosts add significant depth and breadth to the realm of paranormal romance. Their individual characteristics and story arcs allow for a multifaceted exploration of love, longing, sacrifice, and acceptance. This genre, with its dark, thrilling characters and moving love stories, serves to remind us of the timeless allure of love and the lengths we are willing to go in its name.

Chapter 3

More on Fairies, Witches, and other Mythical Beings

Fairies, witches, and other mythical beings inject a potent dose of magic and wonder into the already mesmerizing world of paranormal romance. They bring ancient lore, mystical abilities, and a touch of whimsy, enriching the narrative tapestry with their unique charms and complexities. Weaving these ethereal beings into your love stories opens up a treasure trove of possibilities, allowing you to explore themes of destiny, duality, and the eternal battle between light and darkness.

Fairies, with their gossamer wings and mischievousaura, often embody the capricious nature of magic itself. They can be enchanting allies, bestowing blessings and guiding lost souls, or they can be potent tricksters, weaving illusions and luring unsuspecting humans into their captivating, often perilous, realm. Their ancient origins and deep connection to the natural world provide ample opportunities to craft stories rooted in environmentalism, the balance between human desires and the needs of nature, and the timeless struggle between preservation and exploitation.

Imagine a love story set against a backdrop of an ancient forest threatened by encroaching development, where a human protagonist falls for a captivating fairy sworn to protect their fading magic. Or perhaps your story unfolds in a bustling city where pockets of hidden magic linger, and a chance encounter with a mischievous sprite leads to an unexpected romance. The key is to explore the duality of their nature—the enchanting allure and potential danger—creating captivating tension as your characters navigate their feelings for these beguiling beings.

Witches, on the other hand, embody a different kind of power. Often depicted as wise women, healers, or wielders of formidable magic, witches bring a sense of feminine mystique and strength to paranormal romance. They challenge patriarchal structures and societal norms, embracing their power with confidence and independence. Whether they practice benevolent magic, seeking harmony with nature, or explore darker, forbidden arts, witches offer a rich tapestry of possibilities for crafting compelling narratives.

Consider a love story centered around a coven of witches guarding ancient secrets passed down through generations, their lives intertwined with a prophecy and the arrival of an outsider who ignites a forbidden passion. Or perhaps your narrative focuses on a solitary witch living in a modern city, her magic hidden from the world until a chance encounter with a skeptical detective forces her to reveal her true nature. The key is to showcase their strength, resilience, and unwavering connection to their magic, creating characters who are both relatable and awe-inspiring.

Beyond the well-trodden paths of fairies and witches, the world of mythology brims with lesser-known beings that can add depth and intrigue to your paranormal romances. Shape-shifters, with their ability to traverse different worlds and assume various forms, can introduce themes of identity, transformation, and the fluidity of self. Imagine a love story where a human falls for a mysterious individual hiding a captivating secret—their true nature as a shapeshifter torn between their animalistic instincts and their desire for human connection.

Sirens, often depicted as alluring yet deadly creatures, provide opportunities to explore the seductive power of the unknown and the dangers that come with obsession. Consider a love story where a siren, weary of their solitary existence, finds solace in the arms of a compassionate human who sees past their enchanting facade. The encounter challenges their perception of love and sacrifice, forcing them to confront the consequences of their actions and the potential for redemption.

Djinn, powerful genies bound to fulfill wishes, offer a unique perspective on fate, free will, and the intoxicating allure of having one's deepest desires granted. Imagine a love story that ignites when a human stumbles upon an ancient artifact, unknowingly unleashing a bound djinn who promises to fulfill their heart's desire. As the wish unfolds, complications arise, forcing the characters to navigate the intricate dance between destiny, desire, and the true meaning of happiness.

When incorporating these mythical beings into your paranormal romances, remember to ground them in relatable experiences. Explore their motivations, desires, and vulnerabilities. Just like human characters, they should be driven by longing, seeking connection, purpose, and perhaps even redemption.

Remember, the success of your paranormal romance lies not only in the fantastical elements you incorporate but also in the depth of emotions you evoke. These mythical beings, with their rich history and captivating abilities, serve as powerful catalysts, propelling your characters on journeys of self-discovery, challenging their beliefs, and ultimately leading them to a love that transcends the boundaries of the ordinary.

Chapter 4

World-Building

Creating a paranormal world demands a combination of imagination and discipline. You're not just building a setting, you're breathing life into an entirely new realm like the vividly dark atmosphere of "The Witching Hour". Your world should pull readers in, immersing them in a place where the extraordinary is possible and every detail contributes to the atmosphere. Begin with the senses – the smell of ancient spellbooks, the sight of a towering castle shrouded in mist, the sound of a werewolf's distant howl. Root your world in a tangible reality and then layer the paranormal elements on top, so the transition into the supernatural feels as seamless as walking into a shadow. Just remember, the more fantastical your world, the more anchored your characters' emotional experiences need to be.

The rules and logic of your supernatural elements should be as concrete as the laws of physics in our world. Look at "The Others" series where the abilities and limitations of the terre indigene are clearly set out and integral to the plot. What can your vampires, witches, or werewolves do, and what are their weaknesses? Establish these guidelines early on and adhere to them, because they form the basis of your readers' suspension of disbelief. Inconsistency here can break the spell of your narrative, pulling the reader out of the story. Your creatures' powers should have not only strengths but also costs or consequences, creating a balance that adds tension and stakes to the narrative.

Consistency in your world-building creates a sturdy backbone for your story. Consider the world of "The Bone Season", where the clairvoyant society's hierarchy and rules are clear and consistent, providing a solid stage for the drama to unfold. Map out the geography, politics, and cultures of your world; understanding how these elements interact will help maintain the consistency that readers crave. As with any society, your paranormal world should have history, norms, and an economy that makes sense within its own confines. When these elements are in harmony, they silently uphold the plot, allowing your characters to move through a world that feels lived-in and real. Be meticulous in your creation, and your readers will inhabit your world as unquestioningly as their own.

Your paranormal world should also have a mythology that binds the characters to the setting. The rich lore in "The Grisha Trilogy" anchors the magical elements to the world's history, providing depth and context. Create legends, myths, or prophecies revered within your world, but always leave room for the unknown and the mystical that can evolve with your story. This foundational mythology provides constraints that can organically generate conflict and intrigue within the narrative. It gives characters a shared past to interact with and react against, offering readers a more immersive dive into the world you've crafted. Remember, a fully realized mythology can serve as both a guide and a source of conflict within your tale.

Even in a world where magic exists, there must be a sense of normalcy and routine. In "The Night Circus", the circus operates with its own internal logic amid its enchantments. Consider what constitutes a regular day for your characters —how they interact with their environment, what they eat, how they socialize. This day-to-day reality provides a framework within which the extraordinary events can be juxtaposed, heightening their impact. Readers need this baseline normalcy to understand and appreciate the disruptions caused by the supernatural plot twists. In showing the mundane aspects of your paranormal world, you also ground your readers, providing connection and contrast to their reality.

The supernatural elements should interlace with the romance in a way that feels organic, not forced. The soulmate principle in "The Soulfinders" series is an excellent example where the paranormal aspect of destined love enhances the romantic tension. If your characters are fated to be together, explain why this is so in your world; if they're divided by supernatural barriers, make those barriers real and meaningful. Your paranormal rules can play a pivotal role in character development, relationship dynamics, and conflict – both internal and external. The key is to intertwine these threads so tightly that one cannot exist without the other, making the paranormal part of the romance and the romance part of the paranormal. This is what will give your story its unique flavor and appeal.

Diversity in your world's inhabitants will add richness and complexity to your narrative. "The Shadowhunter Chronicles" feature a variety of supernatural creatures, each with their own cultures and conflicts. Populate your world with a range of beings and think about their relationships with one another—tensions, alliances, prejudices. These dynamics can add layers to your plot and flesh out your world as a place where multiple narratives and histories coalesce. Your characters' attitudes towards and interactions with these groups can also be used to develop their personalities and create a more vibrant tale. Each creature and culture brings a new opportunity to explore different aspects of your paranormal realm.

Even in a paranormal world, there must be consequences for breaking the rules. "The Mercy Thompson" series demonstrates how bending the supernatural laws results in real-world repercussions. This should apply to your characters' use of magic, interactions with other creatures, and engagement with secret societies. The threat of these consequences adds weight to your characters' decisions and heightens the stakes. When readers know that actions have serious repercussions, they become more invested in the characters' choices and the risks they take. Remember that even unlimited power is less interesting than power with price tags and limitations.

Remember that the world outside your paranormal bubble must still exist. In "The Dresden Files", the magical is hidden within the modern city of Chicago, giving readers a real-world anchor. Consider how your world coexists with or hides from normal society. There should be a logical reason in your narrative for why the everyday human population is unaware of the magic around them, or how and why they interact with it. These rules of engagement between the paranormal and the normal determine the level of secrecy or integration in your world, setting the scene for potential conflicts and points of tension in your story.

The economy of your paranormal world should reflect its unique elements. "The Kate Daniels" series does this well by having a fluctuating magic-technology dynamic that affects everyday life and trade. Think about how supernatural elements would impact business, trade, and currency. If magic exists, how is it regulated, traded, or sold? These details not only bolster the believability of your world but can also become major plot points or conflict drivers in your story. They help you consider how characters sustain themselves and what sorts of professions or illegal activities might be common in a world where the paranormal is real.

History plays a crucial role in any world's creation. "The Infernal Devices" unfolds within a rich historical tapestry that frames its paranormal events. Research real historical periods and figures for inspiration, and consider how history has shaped your world's current state. Perhaps there's an ancient war that still casts a long shadow, or historical alliances that dictate today's political climate. Your characters should be products of their world's history, influenced by past events that ripple into the present narrative. By weaving a backstory into your world, you provide context and depth that can influence your main plot in subtle and significant ways.

Religion and belief systems often shape a society and should also be considered in your paranormal world. In "The Stormlight Archive", the characters' belief systems are integral to how they understand and interact with the magical elements around them. Consider how the supernatural aspects of your world might influence its religions and mythologies. These elements will not only affect your characters on a societal level but also on a personal one, as they influence values, behaviors, and worldviews. The complexity added by religious and belief structures will make your world and its inhabitants more realistic and relatable for your readers.

Geography can influence much about your paranormal world, much like the landscape of the Australian outback affects the setting in "Tomorrow, When the War Began". Consider how the physicality of your world shapes your characters' experiences and conditions the plots. Are there certain places where magic is stronger, or locations that are sacred to your paranormal creatures? The layout of the land, the climate, and the biodiversity all contribute to the natural environment in which your story unfolds. It can provide natural barriers, hiding places, and battlegrounds that are unique to your world and crucial for the story.

While building a comprehensive paranormal world, always keep the door open for further exploration and expansion. "The Wheel of Time" series showcases a world that progressively unfolds, densely packed and ever-expanding. As your characters grow and move through the narrative, new corners of your world should reveal themselves, always feeling like they were part of the fabric all along. Be ready to grow and adapt your world alongside your story, knowing that a world with room to breathe is one that can sustain a long and richly told tale. Keep the mystery alive; let your readers feel there is always something more to discover just beyond their current understanding.

Creating a believable and engrossing paranormal world for your romance is a task that requires careful planning and attention to detail. Consistency, logic, and depth are your tools to construct a setting that readers will lose themselves in, time and time again. Building a paranormal world is more than just crafting a backdrop for your story; it's about creating an immersive experience that complements and enriches the journey of your characters. Take the time to lay a solid foundation, and your world, like those in the pages of the bestsellers, will endure long after the last page is turned.

Chapter 5

Themes in Paranormal Romance

Paranormal romance, at its core, thrives on the same compelling themes found in any great love story: the yearning for connection, the joy of discovery, the trials of trust, and the enduring power of love to overcome seemingly insurmountable obstacles. Yet, within the realm of the paranormal, these universal themes take on new dimensions, becoming intertwined with the extraordinary, the magical, and often, the dangerous.

One of the most prevalent themes in paranormal romance is acceptance. This theme manifests in various ways: acceptance of one's true nature, acceptance of a lover's hidden identity, acceptance of a world where the impossible becomes possible. Your characters may struggle to reconcile their human experiences with newfound powers, grapple with the implications of their supernatural heritage, or navigate the complexities of loving someone who exists outside societal norms.

Forbidden love is another cornerstone of the genre, heightened by the extraordinary circumstances surrounding your characters. The inherent "otherness" of paranormal beings often creates societal divides, prejudices, or even ancient laws that threaten to keep lovers apart. The intensity of their connection, the forbidden nature of their desire, becomes a driving force, testing their loyalty, forcing them to make difficult choices, and ultimately, strengthening their bond.

The exploration of duality, the interplay between light and darkness, also takes center stage in many paranormal romances. Your characters may embody this duality within themselves, grappling with their human vulnerabilities alongside their extraordinary abilities, their capacity for love juxtaposed with their potential for destruction. This internal struggle adds depth and complexity to their characters, making their journeys both relatable and captivating.

The theme of destiny often intertwines with the narrative, adding a layer of preordained connection to the burgeoning romance. Prophecies, ancient bloodlines, or soulmate bonds predetermined by fate can create a sense of inevitability, drawing your characters together despite their best intentions or the obstacles that stand in their way. This element of destiny can heighten the stakes, suggesting a love written in the stars while simultaneously challenging your characters to forge their paths.

Redemption serves as a powerful motivator for many paranormal characters, driving their actions and influencing their capacity for love. Vampires seeking atonement for past sins, werewolves struggling to control their primal instincts, or ghosts yearning to right past wrongs provide fertile ground for exploring themes of forgiveness, second chances, and the transformative power of love.

Don't shy away from weaving complex themes into your narrative. Explore the ethical implications of wielding magic, the societal consequences of prejudice against supernatural beings, the bittersweet nature of immortality, or the enduring power of love beyond the grave.

These themes add depth and richness to your love story, elevating it beyond a simple romance and delving into profound questions about identity, purpose, and the complexities of human (and non-human) existence. Remember, your characters' emotional journeys are just as important as the fantastical elements surrounding them.

Show how they grapple with the challenges presented by these themes. Let their vulnerabilities shine through. Allow them to make mistakes, to experience doubt and fear. It's in these moments of raw honesty that your readers will connect with them on a deeper level, becoming invested in their happiness and ultimately, rooting for their love to conquer all.

Don't be afraid to subvert expectations or challenge traditional tropes. Explore the darker side of love, the possessive nature of immortality, the corrupting influence of power, or the heartbreaking consequences of sacrificing one's true self for the sake of another.

Remember, the most compelling paranormal romances stay with readers long after they've finished the last page. They spark conversations, challenge perspectives, and remind us that even in a world where the impossible becomes possible, love remains the most extraordinary magic of all.

Use these themes as springboards for your imagination. Explore them, twist them, and make them your own. By infusing your paranormal romance with thought-provoking themes and emotional depth, you create a reading experience that is both entertaining and profoundly moving.

Chapter 6

Love and Danger

Love and danger are the twin pillars that hold up the world of paranormal romance. The allure of danger adds a thrilling edge to the love story, heightening the stakes and captivating readers with the promise of adrenaline-pumping action and heart-pounding suspense. From vampires whose love is entwined with the risk of bloodlust to witches harnessing forbidden power in the face of peril, the dance between love and danger is a source of tension and excitement in the genre.

In the *Twilight* series by Stephenie Meyer, the love between Bella Swan and Edward Cullen is fraught with danger. Edward's intense hunger for Bella's blood presents a constant threat to her safety, as he fights against his primal instincts. The perilous nature of their love intensifies their romance, driving the narrative and keeping readers on the edge of their seats.

Jeaniene Frost's Night Huntress series also explores the intertwining of love and danger. In the first book, *Halfway to the Grave*, we meet Cat Crawfield, a half-vampire vampire slayer, and Bones, a charismatic vampire with a penchant for danger. Their forbidden romance is imbued with suspense and peril, as they navigate the treacherous world of vampires and battle against powerful enemies.

Danger can also come from external forces, such as the supernatural threats lurking in J.R. Ward's *Black Dagger Brotherhood* series. The warriors of the Black Dagger Brotherhood, fiercely loyal and battle-hardened, find love amidst a world teeming with dangerous creatures. The constant threat of violence and the fight against evil provides a backdrop of danger that underscores the intensity of their romantic relationships.

Laurell K. Hamilton's *Anita Blake* series thrusts the eponymous heroine into a world of danger as she battles supernatural creatures and solves mysteries while navigating complex romantic relationships. The persistent danger that follows Anita adds a layer of tension to her love life, testing the strength of her connections and keeping readers hooked on the edge of their seats.

Danger can take many forms in paranormal romances, from physical threats to emotional turmoil. The villainous presence of the Volturi in the Twilight series exemplifies the external danger that threatens Bella and Edward's love.

The malevolent Fae Court in Karen Marie *Moning's Fever* series keeps her protagonist, MacKayla Lane, in constant peril as she discovers her own powers and falls in love with the enigmatic Jericho Barrons.

In Patricia Briggs' *Mercy Thompson* series, the danger arises from the complex dynamics between werewolves, vampires, and fae, as well as Mercy's own powers as a shapeshifting coyote. Her romantic entanglements, particularly with the werewolf alpha Adam Hauptman, are colored by the risks that come with being involved in a supernatural world.

The allure of danger in paranormal romance lies not only in the external threats characters face but also in the emotional risks they take. This is evident in Kresley Cole's Immortals After Dark series, where the characters must navigate the treacherous landscape of their own emotions amidst dangerous adventures. The sensual tension and emotional vulnerability heighten the intensity of the romantic relationships.

Danger adds a layer of excitement and urgency to the love story in Nalini Singh's Psy-Changeling series. The characters, with their unique psychic and shapeshifting abilities, are often embroiled in life-or-death situations as they fight against powerful enemies and unravel intricate plots. The danger they face bonds them together and tests the strength of their love.

The Bloodlines series by Richelle Mead offers a unique blend of romance and danger as it explores the relationships between humans, vampires, and magic-wielders. The constant threat of violence from anti-vampire groups and the intricate power struggles within the supernatural world heighten the tension in romantic relationships and keep readers engrossed.

In Karen Chance's Cassandra Palmer series, danger is an ever-present companion. Cassandra, a powerful clairvoyant, must navigate complex relationships with vampires, mages, and other supernatural beings while facing off against formidable adversaries. The threat of danger adds a thrilling edge to the romantic entanglements that develop throughout the series.

The blending of love and danger in paranormal romance serves to push characters to their limits, testing their loyalty, courage, and commitment. It spurs them to confront their deepest fears and insecurities, and forces them to make difficult choices that can determine the fate of their relationships.

Through the blending of romantic love and danger, paranormal romance captures the essence of passion and exhilaration. It keeps readers invested in the characters' journeys by offering a high-stakes, emotionally-charged backdrop that showcases the depth of their love and commitment.

The interplay between love and danger is a delicate balance that adds a captivating layer to the genre. By infusing your paranormal romance with danger, whether it be external threats or internal emotional turmoil, you create a dynamic narrative that keeps readers hooked and rooting for the triumph of love over adversity. It's this tantalizing mix of love and danger that keeps readers coming back for more, eager to experience the electrifying ride that paranormal romance offers.

Chapter 7

Role of Conflict between the Normal and Supernatural

In the heart of paranormal romance lies a compelling tension – the clash between the ordinary and the extraordinary, the friction between the human world and the supernatural realm. This conflict provides the fertile ground upon which your love story blooms, creating a captivating backdrop of mystery and intrigue, where characters must navigate a world teetering between the familiar and the fantastic.

The conflict between the ordinary and the extraordinary adds a layer of complexity to your characters' relationships. They may find themselves torn between their human desires and their supernatural obligations, their mundane routines disrupted by extraordinary events, or their love tested by the societal divide between those who embrace the supernatural and those who fear it. This inherent tension becomes the driving force of their journey, compelling them to confront their fears, challenge societal norms, and ultimately, embrace their true identities.

Consider the impact of a vampire falling in love with a human. The vampire's struggle to control their bloodlust, the human's fear of the unknown, and the external threat of prejudice from those who fear vampires create a dramatic backdrop for their love story. The tension between their worlds becomes the central conflict, forcing them to make difficult choices and to fight for their love.

Or imagine a witch trying to hide her magic in a world that fears and misunderstands her gifts. She must balance her natural inclination for power with the desire to blend in, to protect her identity and safety. This internal conflict plays out in her relationships, influencing her choices and coloring her actions.

The conflict between the normal and the supernatural can also manifest as a clash of philosophies and beliefs. The supernatural world may hold its own set of laws, traditions, and morals that clash with the human world's expectations. This tension can lead to misunderstandings, moral dilemmas, and even betrayal, pushing your characters to confront the gray areas between right and wrong.

Take, for instance, the concept of the werewolf's primal instincts clashing with the social expectations of their human pack. The struggle to control their beastly nature, the fear of succumbing to their animalistic urges, and the external pressure to conform to societal norms can create a compelling internal conflict that infuses their love life with complexity and drama.

The "normal" world in your paranormal romance can serve as a source of both comfort and conflict for your characters. It's where they find a sense of normalcy and connection, but it can also be a place of hostility and prejudice towards the supernatural. This creates a constant tension, a feeling of being caught between two worlds, and a longing for acceptance.

For a captivating paranormal romance, you can explore the fear and distrust the two worlds have for each other. This clash extends to those who possess supernatural powers and those who don't. The "normal" world often perceives the supernatural with fear and dread, leading to oppression, persecution, and discrimination.

This creates an environment where your characters must fight for acceptance, not only for their chosen love but also for their very existence. They might be forced to hide their true nature, to live in secrecy, or to constantly defend their right to be themselves.

The conflict between the normal and the supernatural can also be a source of humor. The "normal" world often serves as a foil to the extraordinary, highlighting the incongruities and absurdities that arise when the two collide. Imagine a vampire struggling to blend in with a human world, awkwardly navigating social situations, or a witch grappling with the latest trends in human fashion.

However, the conflict between the normal and the supernatural shouldn't be purely antagonistic. It can also be a source of learning and growth for your characters. Through their interactions with the "normal" world, your supernatural characters may gain a deeper understanding of human values and emotions. Conversely, your human characters can be challenged to embrace the possibilities and potential of a world beyond their comprehension.

Embrace the potential for transformation as your characters engage with the conflict between the normal and the supernatural. A vampire's transformation from a creature of the night to a compassionate lover, a witch's journey from ostracized outsider to a valued member of their community, or a werewolf's ability to find balance between their human and animalistic nature, all highlight the potential for growth and redemption.

Make sure your conflict is more than just a backdrop. Let it be a catalyst for character development. Show how your characters face their fears, make compromises, and learn to embrace the beauty and power of both the normal and the supernatural worlds.

By crafting a compelling narrative that explores the conflict between the ordinary and the extraordinary, you invite readers to explore a nuanced world where love transcends boundaries, where acceptance blooms amidst the tension, and where the characters ultimately find their own unique balance between their human and supernatural identities. This creates a world that resonates deeply with readers, leaving them with a lasting impression of the power of love to conquer even the most formidable differences.

Chapter 8

Examples of Successful Paranormal Romances

Paranormal romance novels have captivated readers for decades, blending elements of the supernatural with heart-pounding romance. One of the most well-known series in this genre is Stephenie Meyer's "Twilight" saga. The story of Bella Swan and Edward Cullen, a human and a vampire, respectively, resonated with millions of readers. What sets this series apart is not just its portrayal of forbidden love but also its exploration of personal sacrifice and the battle between innate desires and moral choices. The series' success lies in its relatable characters, despite their supernatural attributes, and its ability to tap into deep emotions of longing and belonging.

Another standout example is J.R. Ward's "Black Dagger Brotherhood" series, which delves into the lives of warrior vampires. Each book focuses on a different member of the

Brotherhood, blending action-packed battle scenes with intense romantic entanglements. The series' strength is its complex world-building, which immerses readers in a society hidden in plain sight. Ward's ability to create multifaceted characters who struggle with both external threats and internal demons keeps the narrative fresh and engaging. Readers are drawn to the blend of high stakes and heartfelt connections that make each love story unique.

Nalini Singh's "Psy-Changeling" series offers a dive into a futuristic world where psychics, or Psy, coexist with shape-shifters and humans. The series deftly combines sci-fi and paranormal elements, creating a rich tapestry of inter-woven plots and diverse characters. The intense, often volatile, relationships between characters from different factions drive the stories forward, making each book a grip-ping read. Singh's intricate plotlines and meticulous char-acter development ensure that readers are constantly engaged, eagerly anticipating the next twist or romantic development. The powerful themes of identity, accep-tance, and the battle between emotion and logic resonate deeply with readers.

In Charlaine Harris's "Sookie Stackhouse" series, the small-town Southern charm contrasts sharply with the dark, supernatural events that unfold. The protagonist, Sookie, is a telepath navigating a world populated by vampires, were-wolves, and other supernatural beings. Harris's series gains its appeal from the juxtaposition of Sookie's ordinary life with the extraordinary happenings around her. The strong, relatable central heroine, combined with witty dialogue and intricate plot twists, keeps readers hooked. The mix of mystery, romance, and supernatural elements make this series a beloved staple in the paranormal romance genre.

Kresley Cole's "Immortals After Dark" series stands out for its wide array of supernatural beings, including vampires, valkyries, demons, and more. Each installment focuses on a different couple, with their own unique challenges and love stories. Cole's masterful storytelling lies in her ability to weave humor and darkness, creating emotionally charged and adventure-filled narratives. The series' diverse characters and the ever-expanding mythos draw readers into a vividly imagined world where anything is possible. This blend of fantasy, romance, and action-packed story-lines maintains a captivating allure.

"Outlander" by Diana Gabaldon, though straddling the line between historical fiction and paranormal romance, deserves mention for its timeless appeal. The time-traveling love story of Claire Randall and Jamie Fraser has enchanted readers with its rich historical detail and passionate romance. Gabaldon's intricate plotting and deeply researched historical settings lend authenticity to the fantastical elements of time travel. The protagonists' chemistry and the epic scope of their journey through time create a compelling narrative. The blend of history, romance, and the supernatural makes "Outlander" a standout in the genre.

L.J. Smith's "The Vampire Diaries" series is another cornerstone of paranormal romance, highlighting the tumultuous lives of Elena Gilbert and the vampire brothers Damon and Stefan Salvatore. Smith's series is renowned for its dynamic character arcs and emotionally charged love triangles. The series' exploration of themes like redemption, eternal love, and the conflict between good and evil captivates readers. The intense, often dramatic interactions, combined with a fast-paced narrative, ensure that readers are continuously engaged. The blend of romance, suspense, and supernatural intrigue makes it a lasting favorite.

Gena Showalter's "Lords of the Underworld" series brings mythological elements into the paranormal romance fold, featuring immortal warriors cursed by ancient gods. The series is marked by its high-stakes plots and deeply tormented characters seeking redemption and love. Showalter's ability to merge ancient myths with contemporary settings provides a fresh twist on traditional paranormal romance. Each warrior's journey to overcome their curse while finding true love adds emotional depth to the action-packed stories. This unique combination of mythology and romance draws readers into a world where love can conquer even the darkest curses.

Laurell K. Hamilton's "Anita Blake: Vampire Hunter" series blends paranormal romance with urban fantasy and crime thriller elements. The titular character, Anita Blake, is a necromancer and vampire hunter embroiled in romantic entanglements with various supernatural beings. Hamilton's series stands out for its gritty, often dark tone and its complex, morally ambiguous characters. The intricate, multi-layered plotlines keep readers on edge, while the intense romantic relationships add depth to the narrative. The blend of horror, romance, and mystery ensures that the series remains a gripping read.

Karen Marie Moning's "Fever" series introduces readers to a world of Fae, where human and supernatural realms collide. The series follows MacKayla Lane as she navigates a perilous quest through a world filled with dangerous Fae, all while discovering her own hidden powers. Moning's vivid descriptions and richly imagined worlds draw readers into a darkly enchanting narrative. The slow-burning romance and the protagonist's evolution from a naïve girl into a powerful woman keep readers invested. The merging of fantasy, romance, and mystery creates a compelling and addictive series.

Christine Feehan's "Dark" series explores the lives of Carpathians, a near-immortal race with vampire-like traits. Each book features a Carpathian finding their lifemate, with their intense bond providing both strength and vulnerability. Feehan's lush and immersive writing style, combined with her imaginative world-building, offers readers a captivating escape into the supernatural. The series' exploration of enduring love and the struggle between light and dark gives it emotional resonance. The intricate, passionate relationships and high-stakes plots ensure that readers remain entranced.

Richelle Mead's "Vampire Academy" introduces a fresh take on vampire lore, focusing on the lives of students at a hidden academy for guardians and their royal charges. The protagonist, Rose Hathaway, is a strong, independent guardian-in-training whose romantic entanglements add tension and depth to the series. Mead's dynamic character development and the blend of high school drama with supernatural elements set the series apart. The fast-paced action and the complexities of the characters' relationships keep readers engaged. The themes of loyalty, friendship, and forbidden love resonate strongly with fans.

Maggie Stiefvater's "Shiver" trilogy, part of "The Wolves of Mercy Falls" series, explores the tender, bittersweet romance between a human girl and a boy who turns into a wolf. The lyrical prose and atmospheric settings create a deeply emotional and immersive reading experience. Stiefvater's focus on character growth and the impending tragedy of the protagonists' situation makes the romance all the more poignant. The series' exploration of identity, change, and the passage of time resonates deeply with readers. The haunting, beautiful love story stands out in the crowded paranormal romance genre.

Deborah Harkness's "All Souls Trilogy" combines elements of historical fiction, romance, and fantasy, featuring a witch and a vampire brought together by a mysterious manuscript. The protagonist, Diana Bishop, and her vampire counterpart, Matthew Clairmont, navigate a world filled with magical secrets and ancient conspiracies. Harkness's scholarly background enriches the narrative with detailed historical and scientific references, adding depth to the fantasy elements. The intricate plot and the slow-burning romance create a sophisticated, compelling story. The series' blend of academic intrigue and supernatural romance captivates a diverse audience.

Finally, Jeaniene Frost's "Night Huntress" series introduces readers to the fierce, half-vampire heroine, Cat Crawfield, and her vampire lover, Bones. The series is renowned for its sharp wit, steamy romance, and action-packed plots. Frost's ability to balance humor with suspense and romance makes the series incredibly engaging. The chemistry between the protagonists and the evolving, high-stakes storyline keep readers hooked from book to book. The blend of strong female empowerment themes and the supernatural romance ensures the series' lasting popularity.

Chapter 9

Creating Relatable Protagonists

Creating relatable protagonists involves creating characters who, despite their supernatural abilities, exhibit human traits and emotions that readers can connect with. One approach is to give the protagonist a clear, defined personality with strengths and flaws. This makes them feel real and allows readers to see themselves in the character. For example, a vampire with a sharp intellect but a crippling fear of failure can create a compelling dynamic. These traits need to be consistent throughout their actions and decisions, showing growth and development over time. It's important that readers can understand and empathize with their struggles and triumphs.

Backstory plays a crucial role in making them relatable. By giving characters rich backgrounds, filled with past experiences, fears, and dreams, readers can better understand their motivations. Take a witch who discovered her powers after a traumatic childhood event; this history can explain her guarded nature and reluctance to trust others. Such backstories add depth, making characters more three-dimensional and approachable. It also opens up avenues for character growth as they confront past demons. The juxtaposition of their paranormal nature with their very human past helps in grounding them.

A strong main character often needs to display resilience and determination. They face extraordinary challenges, and their ability to navigate these while maintaining their core values makes them admirable. This perseverance, whether in fighting supernatural enemies or dealing with personal doubts, endears them to readers. Their journey should be fraught with obstacles that test their limits, showing both their vulnerabilities and their strengths. This balance creates a nuanced character who is capable and relatable. The protagonist's resilience inspires readers while making them more connected to the character's journey.

It's important to showcase the protagonists' emotional spectrum. Despite their supernatural traits, they should experience love, fear, loneliness, and joy just like any human. For instance, a shape-shifter struggling with their dual identity might fear not being accepted by either community. This inner turmoil provides rich material for emotional scenes that resonate with readers. By being transparent about their feelings and reactions to various situations, characters become more accessible. This emotional honesty bridges the gap between the fantastical and the real.

A strong main character also demonstrates empathy and the capacity to form deep connections with others. Characters who show compassion towards friends, family, or even strangers, reveal their humanity. This trait can be depicted through small, everyday actions or significant, selfless deeds, making them admirable. An angel who risks their own safety to save a human, showing their internal conflict over such choices, can deepen their relatability. These interactions build a network of relationships that enrich the narrative. Readers often relate to characters who show they care about others, even in a world filled with supernatural peril.

One of the key traits of strong protagonists is their ability to grow and evolve. A compelling character arc where the protagonist learns from their experiences and becomes stronger or wiser is crucial. This transformation need not always be positive, but it should be meaningful and earned. For example, a demon hunter who starts off reckless but learns to value teamwork and strategy showcases personal growth. This evolution should be evident in their actions, decisions, and interactions with other characters. A well-rounded character arc keeps readers invested in the protagonist's journey from start to finish.

Making protagonists face everyday issues alongside their supernatural challenges helps ground them in reality. Balancing a dual life, dealing with family expectations, or managing a romantic relationship amidst supernatural chaos can make them more relatable. A ghost whisperer who struggles to maintain her day job while dealing with spirits offers a blend of the mundane and the extraordinary. Readers can see reflections of their own lives in these everyday struggles, making the protagonist more accessible. This blending of normalcy with the paranormal creates a richer, more immersive experience.

Humor is another valuable trait that can make protagonists more relatable. Infusing a character with a sense of humor, especially in dire situations, humanizes them. It shows their ability to maintain perspective and cope with stress, qualities that many readers admire. A vampire who makes light-hearted jokes about their fangs or a witch who uses sarcasm to mask their fear can add a refreshing layer to their personality. This levity can provide relief from intense plot moments and make characters more likable. It creates a bond where readers not only admire but also enjoy spending time with the protagonist.

A strong protagonist also requires a clear sense of agency. They should be active participants in their story, making choices that drive the plot forward rather than merely reacting to events. This sense of control and determination makes them admirable and compelling. For instance, a protagonist who takes charge in solving a mystery involving supernatural occurrences shows leadership and initiative. Readers are drawn to characters who shape their destinies through their actions. This proactive nature enhances the character's strength and relatability.

It's also important for protagonists to exhibit moral complexity. Characters with black-and-white morality can seem unrealistic and less engaging. Instead, a werewolf who struggles with their violent instincts while striving to do good provides a rich moral canvas. This internal conflict resonates with readers who understand that real life often involves navigating shades of gray. Showing characters making tough, nuanced decisions makes them more human. This complexity deepens the narrative and enhances the reader's connection to the protagonist.

Protagonists often have clear personal goals and stakes. Having something at risk, whether it's a loved one, a cherished position, or their own soul, can make readers root for them. For example, a fallen angel seeking redemption adds emotional weight to their journey. The more personal and high-stakes their goals, the more invested readers become. Clearly defined stakes also help in structuring the plot and pacing, giving the story momentum. As readers understand what drives the protagonist, they feel more connected and concerned about their outcomes.

A protagonist's interactions with secondary characters can also enhance their relatability. By showing how they engage in friendships, rivalries, and mentorships, writers can flesh out their personality. A witch who has a supportive yet complicated relationship with her non-magical sibling adds layers to her character. These relationships can reflect the protagonist's inner world and highlight different facets of their personality. Interactions that are natural and multi-dimensional help in constructing a realistic and relatable character. It shows that even in a supernatural context, they experience relationships similarly to the readers.

Overcoming personal fears is another way to create relatable protagonists. Everyone has fears, and showing a character confronting and dealing with their own can resonate deeply. A ghost hunter who confronts their fear of losing their loved ones while facing dangerous specters adds an emotional undercurrent. This fear provides motivation and makes their courage more authentic. Readers appreciate characters who show bravery in the face of their deepest fears. This makes the protagonist's victories more impactful and their character more inspiring.

These protagonists often have hobbies or interests outside their supernatural duties, which humanize them. Whether they enjoy painting, gardening, cooking, or reading, these interests make them more three-dimensional. A shape-shifter who loves cooking Italian cuisine adds a charming, relatable layer to their character. These hobbies can offer moments of warmth and normalcy amidst the high tension of paranormal activities. It shows that despite their extraordinary abilities, they engage in ordinary pleasures. This blend of the extraordinary and the ordinary helps readers connect on a personal level.

Lastly, protagonists who exhibit self-awareness and growth reflect a realistic, relatable journey. Characters that recognize their flaws and work towards improving them resonate with readers. A vampire acknowledging their isolation and making efforts to form genuine bonds shows maturity. This added layer of self-improvement and reflection makes the character's journey feel authentic. Readers are often inspired by characters who strive to better themselves. This growth mirrors the reader's own life journey, making the connection to the protagonist more profound.

Chapter 10

Pick your Paranormal Being (Examples)

Sirens stand out with their hauntingly beautiful voices. These creatures, who can trace their roots to ancient Greek mythology, have the unique ability to lure sailors to their doom with their captivating songs. However, it's not just any melody they sing; their voices carry a magical frequency that resonates with the human psyche, pulling at the strings of desire and curiosity. Unlike their mythological counterparts, modern Sirens blend into society, often found as exceptional singers or performers. Their power is not in their malevolence, but in the ability to influence emotions and decisions, which they use judiciously, aware of the responsibility that comes with such an ability. They maintain a mysterious air, often choosing isolation over society, to protect themselves and others from the potent effects of their gift.

The lore of the **werewolf** has been around for centuries, often depicting these beings as monstrous and uncontrollable. However, the werewolves of today have evolved. They possess an acute sense of smell, far superior to any human or animal, which allows them to detect even the slightest changes in their environment. They have a connection to the moon, which heralds their transformation, but it is not the full moon that triggers the change; rather, it is their emotional state. These beings can control their transformations with rigorous discipline and self-awareness. Their struggle to balance the wild nature with their human side becomes a testament to their resilience, making them not mindless beasts, but guardians of the balance between man and nature.

Vampires, once feared as night stalkers and bloodthirsty monsters, have a more nuanced existence in the world today. They do require blood to survive, but many have turned to animal blood or synthetic alternatives to avoid harming humans. What makes them particularly fascinating is their ability to heal rapidly from almost any wound, making them nearly immortal. They are also known for their charisma and persuasive abilities, which they use to blend into society and often rise to positions of influence. However, they are sensitive to sunlight, not because it burns them to ash, but because it affects their regenerative abilities and weakens them significantly. Vampires have a rich culture and history, with many dedicating themselves to preserving their heritage and coexisting with humanity under strict ethical guidelines.

Ghosts, the ethereal entities that are often the center of horror stories, are in reality echoes of the past. They are not always the restless spirits of the dead, but residual energy that remains in places with a strong emotional imprint. Their ability to interact with the physical world is limited, and when they do, it is often through manipulating electromagnetic fields. Some are not even aware they are dead, repeating the same patterns as in life. Others possess a certain level of consciousness and can communicate with the living, usually through mediums. Their presence is not always malevolent; in fact, many seek closure or aim to pass on an important message before they can move on.

The Djinn, or genies, are often misunderstood beings that come from Arabian and Islamic mythology. They have the power to manipulate energy and matter, granting wishes with a precision that often comes with unexpected consequences. Known for their intelligence, they are bound by a code that prevents them from causing direct harm, despite the popular belief that they revel in trickery. Djinn live in a parallel dimension, venturing into our world only when summoned. They connect with humans on a level that transcends language, understanding desires and fears at their core. While they are capable of great feats, their interactions with humans are governed by complex rules, and they maintain a neutral stance in the cosmic balance of good and evil.

Elementals are beings that embody the forces of nature. These spirits have command over natural elements—earth, air, fire, and water. They are typically invisible to the human eye, but their impact is felt in the form of natural phenomena. For instance, a fire elemental might be behind a sudden, inexplicable blaze in a forest, while a water elemental could influence the ebb and flow of tides. Their abilities are directly connected to their emotional state, akin to the temperament of the element they represent. While not inherently malicious, they can be formidable if the natural order they are attuned to is disrupted.

The Fae, or fairies, are often portrayed as whimsical, but they are actually beings of great power and structure. They have a natural affinity with the flora and fauna, being able to communicate and influence plant growth and animal behavior. Some are so in tune with the natural world that they can become invisible within it, camou-flaged perfectly among the leaves and branches. The Fae follow a strict code of conduct known as the Faerie Etiquette, which governs their dealings with each other and the outside world. Though they can appear childlike, they are ancient beings with a sagacity that rivals the oldest of human scholars. They prefer to remain unseen, intervening in human affairs only when the balance of nature is at stake.

Shapeshifters are a diverse group, with the ability to alter their physical form at will. This isn't limited to mimicking human appearance; they can take the form of any creature they have seen, though the transformation requires a deep understanding of the creature's physiology. Their real form is a conundrum, as they are born with this ability and their true appearance is a choice rather than a default. They value freedom above all, and their society lacks the rigid hierarchies found in the human world. Their rare ability makes them invaluable as spies or ambassadors, though most shapeshifters prefer to remain out of political affairs. Their shape-shifting also allows them to heal by reforming their bodies, making them elusive and hard to capture.

The Phoenix, a being of legend, is recognized for its cycle of bursting into flames and rising anew from the ashes. However, in reality, this creature has a unique interaction with fire, able to absorb and control it without harm. The Phoenix has a lifespan that spans centuries, and when it 'dies,' it goes through a process of regeneration, which is less dramatic than the myths suggest. It embodies themes of renewal and resilience, often being sought after for its supposed ability to grant eternal life. However, the Phoenix avoids human interaction, as its power can be as dangerous as it is wondrous. The creature is seen as a symbol of hope and rebirth, a reminder that from the end can come a new beginning.

Nymphs, often associated with specific natural landmarks like rivers, trees, or mountains, are custodians of these natural wonders. Their ability lies in fostering and protecting the vitality of their chosen domain. Nymphs can cause flowers to bloom instantaneously or cleanse a stream with a mere touch. They can communicate with the spirits of their domain, whether it be animals, plants, or the elements themselves. Far from being simple forest dwellers, they act as mediators in the balance of ecosystems. Their continued existence is a barometer for the health of our planet, and as such, they feel the pains of ecological damage more acutely than any other creature.

Specters are a rare form of ethereal being, often confused with ghosts, but distinct in their purpose and abilities. They are the watchers of time, able to observe events from the past and, to a limited extent, possible futures. Specters have no physical form and can pass through walls and objects. Their presence is often felt as a sudden drop in temperature or an inexplicable feeling of being watched. They do not interact with the living, but their silent vigil serves as a constant reminder of the flow of time and the impermanence of all things. They are detached from the emotional spectrum, allowing them to witness without bias or intervention.

The Griffons are majestic creatures with the body of a lion and the wings and head of an eagle. They are known as the guardians of treasures and ancient sites. Their eyesight is unparalleled, able to spot an intruder from miles away. They possess a noble demeanor and follow a strict personal code of honor. Despite their intimidating appearance, Griffons are intelligent and can understand human speech, although they cannot speak it. Their role as protectors extends beyond material treasures; they are often seen as symbols of the protection of knowledge and history.

Sorcerers, though often lumped in with paranormal beings, are mostly human, set apart by their unique affinity for manipulating the energies of the world. Their abilities are honed through study and practice rather than inherent power. They can cast illusions, shift energies, and even perceive the threads that connect living beings. The true sorcerer seeks harmony with the forces they wield, as they understand the destructive potential of their power if left unchecked. Their knowledge of ancient languages and rituals grants them access to resources beyond the scope of modern science. Often, they are the bridge between the human and the paranormal, understanding both worlds and striving to maintain balance.

The Gargoyles, though seen as mere stone statues adorning ancient buildings, are in fact living creatures. They stay motionless during the day, merging with the architecture they are part of, but at night they awaken. Their duty is to ward off evil spirits and protect the premises. Gargoyles possess incredible strength and are formidable combatants. Though they are bound to their edifice, their understanding of the human condition is profound. Their existence is a blend of myth and material, reinforcing the idea that sometimes, guardians come in the most unexpected of forms.

The Merfolk, dwellers of the deep oceans, are an elegant amalgamation of human and fish. They can breathe underwater and swim with the swiftness of the fastest marine animals. Their singing voices are often mistaken for those of the Sirens, but the Merfolk use their voices to communicate and navigate the dark depths of the ocean. They have a deep empathy for sea life and work to maintain the delicate balance of marine ecosystems. Due to the pollution and dangers posed by modern human activities, they have become wary of the surface world. Though they are less frequently seen than in days of old, their legend continues to captivate the hearts of sailors and land dwellers alike.

Living shadows, known as Umbrae, are another breed of paranormal entities that fascinate and terrify.

These beings exist on the fringes of our vision, slipping through cracks in reality like oil through water. They influence dreams and feed on the fears that manifest within them. Their form is evanescent, often seen as a fleeting glimpse out of the corner of one's eye. Umbraes' interaction with the physical world is minimal, leaving only a chill or a sense of unease as evidence of their passing. They embody the unknown facets of the world, the hidden fears and the unexplained phenomena that are attributed to the darkness.

Then there are the **Ephemerals,** beings that exist in moments of beauty and fragility. They are found in the bloom of a rare flower or the fleeting beauty of a sunset. Their power is not in strength or endurance, but in those transient moments that capture the essence of wonder. Ephemerals serve as a reminder to cherish the now, for like their existence, it is passing and precious. They cannot be grasped or contained, and their attempt to do so can cause them to vanish. These beings are the embodiment of the ephemeral nature of life and its inherent beauty.

The Banshees, based on Irish legend, have a presence that is as poignant as it is feared. Their cries are not just harbingers of death, but a lament for the sorrow of loss. They are deeply empathetic beings, connected to the families they follow, and their wails carry the weight of the impending grief. Banshees do not cause death; rather, they are its mournful companions, connecting the world of the living to the beyond. Their visibility to those about to experience a loss is both a gift and a curse, offering a chance for final goodbyes or a painful omen.

Cryptids such as the famous Bigfoot or Yeti are earthbound creatures that defy conventional science. Witnesses describe them as incredibly elusive, with an intelligence that allows them to avoid contact with humans. Their physical prowess is unmatched in the animal kingdom, capable of surviving in the harshest of environments. Though often depicted as savage beasts, reports suggest they exhibit a strong sense of family and social structure. The existence of such creatures raises questions about evolution and our understanding of the natural world. They are a reminder of the vast, unexplored wilderness and the secrets it may hold.

The Timeless, a rare group of beings whose existence spans the flow of history. They are immortal not by nature, but through an intimate knowledge of time and its workings. They can witness the rise and fall of civilizations, the birth and death of stars, without aging a day. While they cannot change significant historical events, they can nudge the course of personal lives in subtle ways. The Timeless epitomize the infinite journey of learning and the possibilities that lie within the folds of eternity. Their interaction with humankind is cautious, as their knowledge is both a priceless treasure and a potential curse.

The Aetherborn are said to be the offspring of stars and cosmos. They traverse the celestial pathways, harmonizing the energies of the universe. Their touch is said to heal the soul, and their presence brings a sense of peace that is almost otherworldly. They are beings of light and energy, rarely taking a form that is understandable to the human sense. Their understanding of existence is vast, yet they are bound by cosmic laws that prevent them from revealing too much to mortals. The Aetherborn are a testament to the beauty and mystery of the universe, a bridge between the finite and the infinite.

Then there are the **Legends**, beings born from the collective belief and storytelling of humanity. They are as diverse as the cultures that create them, ranging from heroes that embody virtues to monsters that carry warnings. Their abilities and strength are directly influenced by the power of their tales and the faith people put in them. They are the living narratives of humanity, walking embodiments of fears, hopes, and morals. Their existence is intangible, yet their impact on human civilization is undeniable, shaping the way societies understand and convey their worldviews.

The Arcanists are beings steeped in the very essence of magic. Their understanding of the arcane arts allows them to cast spells and weave enchantments that defy logic. They are the scholars of the hidden realities, guardians of ancient tomes, and practitioners of forgotten rituals. Despite their potent abilities, they follow a strict code, understanding that with great power comes great responsibility. Their presence is a rare phenomenon, and an encounter with an Arcanist often marks a significant turning point in one's life.

Protectors of the threshold, the **Sentinels** stand guard at the boundaries of worlds, dimensions, and realities. These stalwart guardians exist to maintain the balance between realms, preventing catastrophic overlaps and invasions. They possess the ability to sense fluctuations in the fabric of reality and respond to threats that most beings would not even be aware of. Often depicted with multiple eyes or forms that mirror their domain, the Sentinels serve as both warning and shield against the unknown.

The **Dreamweavers** are artisans of the subconscious, sculptors of the dreamscape. They can craft vivid experiences within the minds of sleepers, weaving dreams with purposes that range from healing traumas to inspiring revelations. Their work is subtle, and most people are unaware of their influence upon waking. The Dreamweavers themselves exist in a state that is neither fully awake nor asleep, constantly balanced on the edge of consciousness. They are both artists and therapists, deeply compassionate and sensitive to the human condition.

Within the seas, there exist the **Leviathans** - colossal beings that embody the might and mystery of the ocean depths. Often misconstrued as mere sea monsters, they are actually intelligent entities, ancient and venerable. Their sheer size allows them to influence the ocean currents and weather patterns. They carry within them the history of the waters they inhabit, and experiences that span hundreds, if not thousands of years. Their interaction with humanity is minimal, as they are content with the solace of the deep and the company of the ocean's song.

Then there is the rare breed of beings known as the **Arbiters.** They are the unseen judges, the weighers of souls and the evaluators of moral balance. Unlike the grim reaper who is a mere escort to the afterlife, the Arbiters determine the merit of one's deeds. They are incorruptible, impartial, and execute their duties with stoic detachment. Their existence nods to the universal longing for justice and the hope that, in the end, all will be held accountable.

In the lush green canopies of the world's rainforests, one may find the **Myriad** - shapeshifting entities with the ability to become any creature of the forest. Their mastery of transformation is so complete that not only their appearance but also their internal biology can match that of the new form. They are the protectors of biodiversity, showcasing the value of every creature, big or small. The Myriad live in the present, adapting and evolving, they symbolize the ever-changing tapestry of life on Earth.

High in the uncharted peaks, the **Skyherds** shepherd the clouds and weather patterns across the globe. With a wave of their hands, they can gather storms or clear the skies. They personify the free spirit of the winds and the untamed power of the skies. Contrary to their immense influence on the weather, the Skyherds are gentle and meditative, mindful of the impact their actions have on the world below.

The Custodians, ancient beings that watch over the sacred sites of the Earth. They are bound to places of power - ancient forests, deep caverns, or hallowed ruins - acting as both guardians and conduits of the energies that flow through these mystical spots. They carry within them the memories of the Earth itself, from its fiery birth to the present day. The Custodians are stoic, often immobile, resembling the statues or totems found at these sacred sites, yet their alert eyes miss nothing, and their commitment to their charge is unwavering.

Chapter 11

Writing Romantic Scenes

Writing romantic scenes is about more than just the physical interaction between characters; it's about capturing the electric charge of attraction that zips through the air when two potential lovers meet. Every glance, every touch, every hesitant smile is loaded with possibility, and it's your job to translate that tension onto the page. Pay attention to the smallest details—the way a hand might shake slightly when touching skin, the catch in a voice, the heat that floods the cheeks. These moments should feel as intimate to the reader as they are to the characters. Let the environment around them fade so that in that moment, they are the only two people in existence, and the air between them is thick with the unspoken.

Building romantic tension is a delicate process, a careful balance between disclosure and secrecy, need and restraint. Like pieces on a chess board, your characters should move towards and away from each other, each action sparking an equal and compelling reaction. They share secrets, exchange lingering looks, and navigate around unspoken emotions which only serve to draw them closer with every encounter. The world around them may sense the heat of their chemistry, but true tension lies in what they keep from the world and each other. Play with proximity, metaphorical and literal, drawing your characters close enough to feel the gravity between them before pulling them apart once more.

The slow burn romance is a smoldering ember that you as the author must coax into a flame with the utmost patience. The long, lingering buildup, where every conversation and glance is a stoke to the fire, creates an investment in the relationship that's as deep for the reader as it is for your characters. Contrastingly, instant attraction strikes like lightning—a powerful, immediate force that can both enthrall and terrify in its intensity. Both have their place in the canvas of your narrative, but it's important to decide early which will more effectively serve your story and your characters. The choice between a slow burn and an instant attraction shapes the structure of the romance and how it intertwines with the paranormal elements you're weaving alongside it.

Creating emotional depth in a romance requires delving into the heart of your characters. It's found in the vulnerability they show and the emotional risks they take. Every fear, hope, and dream they share adds layers to your canvas, painting a love with dimensions and textures that readers can feel. Let moments of weakness and strength define their connection. A laugh shared in the midst of grief, a hand reached out in the dark, a secret entrusted—all these are brushstrokes that contribute to the depth of their bond. Crafting emotional depth isn't just about showing feelings but highlighting change—how love morphs them, softens edges, opens eyes, and, above all, how it heals and hurts.

Writing intimate moments isn't merely about the physical —it's about capturing the chemistry and connection that transcend the corporeal. These scenes should unfurl naturally, each touch and word a testament to the characters' growing relationship. Put focus on the senses—how the air changes, how the simple contact can feel like a shock of electricity, how time seems to dilate. Intimacy isn't always found in grand gestures; sometimes, it's in the shared quiet, an understanding glance, a choice that speaks louder than words. Remember, the essence of intimacy is not in the action itself, but in the atmosphere you create around it—the trust, the emotional connectivity, and the raw humanity shared.

Balancing romance with paranormal elements requires a dance between the real and the otherworldly. The supernatural can be a metaphor for the uncontrollable forces of love—an external embodiment of the turmoil that your characters feel within. Allow the paranormal aspect to challenge the romance, to bring characters together or pull them apart, but never let it outshine the connection that lies at the heart of your story. Like sunlight through leaves, the paranormal should dapple your romantic scenes, casting interesting patterns and colors but not obscuring the view. Equilibrium is key—let the magical enhance the emotional, weaving an intricate pattern that leaves readers entranced by both.

Making scenes feel authentic involves infusing your writing with genuine human emotion and experience. Your characters should react as real people do—they stumble over words, they feel embarrassment, they wallow in the blissful silences. Don't shy away from the messiness of love and connection; embrace it as it adds credibility and relatability to your romance. Even in a world of fantastic creatures and powers, the heart's longings, jealousies, and joys remain unchanged. Let these emotions drive the actions and reactions of your characters, keeping the authentically human at the core of every paranormal encounter.

Dialogue in romantic scenes should ebb and flow with the natural rhythm of conversation punctuated by the characters' emotional states. It's in this back-and-forth where the spark between characters ignites—a teasing remark, a shared revelation, a vulnerable question. Each line of dialogue carries weight, making silences as potent as the words spoken. Let the unspoken linger between your characters; sometimes a pause, a held breath, can speak louder than any confession. Use dialogue to peel back the layers between characters, revealing hearts ready or reluctant for love.

Natural and engaging conversations in romantic scenes reveal as much about the characters as the plot itself. The words exchanged can be playful banter, loaded with subtext, or soft words charged with meaning, yet they always add to the understanding of the relationship. The things they choose to share, and how they share them, reflect their evolving trust and the deepening of their bond. The dialogue should feel true to the characters—resonant with their backstories and consistent with the voice you've crafted for them. Through their conversations, allow them insight into each other's minds and hearts, drawing the reader deeper into their world.

Using dialogue to build connection is an art form. Every exchange is an opportunity for characters to reveal a little more about themselves, to peel back a layer of their carefully constructed walls. Let your characters listen to each other, truly listen, hearing the words said and unsaid. The moments when a protagonist understands what their lover hasn't spoken aloud are just as poignant as any declarations of love. Use dialogue not only to spark or deepen attraction but to show the growing partnership and respect between characters, laying the foundation for a love that feels both inevitable yet hard-earned.

Avoiding clichés in romantic exchanges keeps the interaction fresh and captivating. Resist falling into the trap of overused endearments or grand declarations of love that have lost their luster. Instead, find new ways to express affection tailored to your characters' unique personalities and situations. A scientist might express love in terms of chemical reactions, a warrior might show it through the lengths they'll go to protect, a ghost might whisper it through remnants of their past life. Steering clear of clichés means finding original expressions of love that resonate with your characters' unique voices and experiences.

Fresh and original romantic interactions set your paranormal romance apart from the rest. These are the moments etched into your reader's memory: impromptu dance in a rainstorm, a shared secret underneath a blanket of stars, a kiss that conveys years of longing. Let creativity be your guide; find inspiration in the quirks and histories of your characters, and let their personalities shape these interactions. Originality springs from authenticity—the more grounded in their individualities, the more unique their interactions will be.

Steering clear of overused tropes involves revisiting the familiar with new eyes. If your characters must face the 'forbidden love' scenario, twist it—make the reasons for the taboo fresh, the consequences more dire, or the emotions more nuanced. Challenge yourself to transform the expected narrative beats with innovative encounters and obstacles that feel specific to your world and your characters. Your romance should not just captivate but resonate with originality, rewriting the usual with a pen dipped in the unfamiliar.

The emotional impact of a love story relies on the journey more than the destination. It's not merely about two characters ending up together, but about the hurdles they've crossed to reach that unity. Craft each scene with the intention of leaving a mark on the reader's heart; make them fight with the characters, cry with them, yearn with them. The emotional impact comes from the connection the readers feel with the characters, pushed and pulled by the love that unfolds on the pages. When readers close your book, it's the emotional echo that will linger, the reverberation of the struggle, the sweetness, and the sacrifice that love has exacted.

Making readers feel the romance is about allowing them to experience every moment of hesitation, desire, and affection along with the characters. Draw out sensory details— the brush of fingertips, the shared warmth under a blanket, the racing of heartbeats in a quiet room. Do not rush these encounters; let them build slowly, simmering with tension until the moment of release. And when conflict arises, as it must, delve into the pain with as much attention as the joy. Paint every scene with the hues of the characters' innermost emotions, and your readers will paint their days with thoughts of your story.

Using emotions to drive the story ensures that the romance doesn't just complement the plot—it propels it. The fears, insecurities, and passions of your characters should spur them to action, molding their choices and altering their paths. The emotional journey is the pulse of your narrative, giving life to both the paranormal and the everyday aspects of your world. Allow the emotional currents to guide the story's progression, keeping the beats of romance at the forefront, the stakes personal, and the reader invested. When emotions fuel the story, every twist, every turn carries weight—an emotional gravitas that resonates in the fabric of your tale.

Chapter 12

Romantic Chemistry

Romantic chemistry can ignite in the shared silence between two characters—a moment loaded with unspoken words and unacted desires. Think of the charged quietude in "The Shape of Water", where Elisa and the Amphibian Man communicate through glass, their hands mirroring each other with no words exchanged. There's an electric current in those silent communications, the weight of words not needed, where eyes say everything. Your characters might be separated by a language barrier, social norms, or even species as they are in this tale, but their connection transcends these divides. It's this unspoken understanding that fans the flames of chemistry.

Chemistry often blooms in the witty exchange of banter, the dance of words that act as the characters' verbal fencing. In "Pride and Prejudice", Elizabeth and Mr. Darcy spar with dialogue that cuts to the core, revealing layers of attraction beneath the surface. Each jab and parry pulls them unintentionally closer, their intellectual compatibility fueling a fire that's rooted in respect. As the author, use this repartee to show their mental congruity, allowing their words to caress and clash in equal measure, stoking the embers of a romance that burns slowly but intensely.

Consider the chemistry that forms through shared adversity. When characters are thrust together by external forces, as Katniss and Peeta are in "The Hunger Games", their reliance on one another breeds a unique bond. Through the trials they face, an understanding forms—a recognition of strength, courage, and mutual respect. Their unity against common foes becomes a melting pot for their chemistry, simmering beneath the surface until it's ripe to emerge. Let the struggles they face weave them closer, binding their souls in the crucible of hardship and shared purpose.

Romantic chemistry can spark through a character's selflessness—the moment when one puts the other's needs before their own. This is seen in "Me Before You", as Louisa makes it her mission to show Will a life worth living. As you write such selfless acts into your narrative, they become the kindling for a deeper connection. It silently solidifies a reciprocal appreciation and care that goes beyond attraction, speaking directly to the essence of love. These acts need not be grandiose; the simplest gesture of understanding or sacrifice can ignite a profound affinity between characters.

The tension of unfulfilled longing can be the strongest catalyst for romantic chemistry. In "Outlander", Claire and Jamie's early relationship is marked by the ache of unspoken feelings and societal barriers that keep them apart. The intensity of their unfulfilled desires creates a magnetic force that pulls them—and readers—inevitably together. In your writing, allow the undercurrent of this tension to ebb and flow, teasing out the longing until it becomes almost a tangible entity within the narrative thread. Use longing as a propellant for the plot, drawing characters into situations where the tension thickens and their chemistry becomes unavoidable.

Sometimes, chemistry is rooted in contradiction—the play of opposites that both repel and attract. In "Warm Bodies", we see the unlikely affection blossom between a human and a zombie, their differences creating a dynamic interplay of fear and fascination. The juxtaposition of your characters' contrasts—be it in personality, life goals, or supernatural status—serves to heighten their chemistry, making every shared moment crackle with the tension of reconciliation. Make the unlikely pairing work by highlighting the ways in which they complement each other, the puzzle pieces that fit despite the odds.

Shared passions often become the kindling for romantic chemistry. In "The Rosie Project", it is mutual interest in genetics and an unorthodox approach to finding love that draws the characters together. When your characters share a hobby, a passion, or a quest, it creates a common ground upon which the seeds of attraction can grow. Let their shared interests be the canvas, and their growing affection the intricate pattern painted across it—each shared experience, a brush stroke of color and light that brings their chemistry into vivid picture.

The process of overcoming prejudices or preconceived notions can also forge indelible chemistry. As Darcy and Elizabeth demonstrate in "Pride and Prejudice", their initial disdain gives way to a begrudging respect, and eventually, a deep, burning love. Channel this transformative energy in your writing, allowing your characters to grow through their interactions, challenging each other's worldviews and thus, entwining their lives. This transformation lays bare the very essence of your characters, and in that vulnerability, the undeniable chemistry emerges—a phoenix rising from the ashes of what once was antipathy.

Moments of unexpected tenderness often reveal the depth of a growing chemistry. In "Tell the Wolves I'm Home", it's a moment of shared grief and soft understanding that brings the protagonists closer. Craft scenes where a tough character shows gentleness unexpectedly, or a lighthearted character reveals a depth of seriousness. These breaks from their established personas are like cracks in a dam, allowing a flood of authentic connection and unexpected chemistry to rush through. This allows readers to peek behind the curtain of your characters' facades, revealing the potential for genuine connection.

The thrill of the forbidden or taboo can serve as a formidable source of chemistry. Take "The Vampire Diaries", where the love between a vampire and a human is fraught with danger and societal disapproval—a veritable modern-day star-crossed love. As their forbidden affection threads through your story, it carries with it an edge, a sense of urgency and defiance that is intoxicating. Let their stolen moments feel charged with the weight of consequence, but also with the ecstasy of rebellion, knitting your characters together in a romance that feels both ill-fated and irresistible.

Mutual vulnerability breeds romantic chemistry, as seen when characters see each other at their weakest and still find strength. In "A Court of Thorns and Roses", Feyre and Tamlin's bond strengthens through mutual hardship and shared secrets. Allow your characters' weakest moments to be the crucible for their connection, for it's in the unveiling of one's true self that love finds a foothold. Allow them to witness each other's fears, dreams, and insecurities; it is in these raw exposures that a profound and unyielding chemistry can be forged.

Romantic chemistry also thrives on the thrill of the chase. Like the charged pursuit between Cat and Bones in "Halfway to the Grave", the intensity of pursuit creates an addictive tension. Whether it's a playful dance around feelings or a dangerous game of evasion, the thrill lies within the chase itself. Keep your readers guessing, alloying the draw of 'will they, won't they' with the spark of danger or the promise of an otherworldly love. The chase heightens attraction, fuels passion, and lays the groundwork for a connection that's exciting for its unpredictability.

Tracing the origins of romantic chemistry can be as fascinating as the chemistry itself. In "The Night Circus", the protagonists are drawn together not just by affection, but by an entangled destiny woven long before their meeting. This fated pull, a path crossing as if mapped in the stars, can be a powerful driver of chemistry. In your writing, imbue their every interaction with a sense of inevitability—an alignment of cosmic forces or ancient spells that ties them as surely as any vow.

Chemistry sometimes ignites in the embers of a long-standing friendship, as seen in "Friends Without Benefits". This slow burn comes from a foundation built not only on mutual affection but on history and deep-seated trust.

Their shared past adds layers to their bond, and when romantic feelings surface, they're not just spontaneous sparks but the fanning of flames long smoldering. Portray your characters' friendship as the bedrock upon which their newfound romance is built, a tie that weathers the storm of changing emotions, sculpting a chemistry that feels enduring and real.

Subtle gestures often speak louder than the overt in terms of romantic chemistry. Think of "Eleanor & Park" where the simple act of holding hands becomes a profound connection between the two protagonists. These are moments laden with meaning—the brushing of shoulders, a lingering gaze, the shared breath of laughter. As your characters navigate their world, let these tender, unassuming moments become milestones in their romantic journey. These instances are the threads of silver woven through the tapelet of their burgeoning love story.

Chapter 13

Character ARCs

Your characters' arcs are the spine of your paranormal romance, giving it structure and support. As in "The Night Circus" by Erin Morgenstern, where Celia and Marco grow from pawns in a game to masters of their own fate, your characters should start in one place and end in another, both physically and emotionally. Give them a clear internal flaw or external challenge at the beginning that they must face and eventually overcome. This journey should be fraught with both personal challenges and paranormal obstacles, forging them in the fire of their own story. As they evolve, these changes should be clear but gradual, surprising yet inevitable when readers look back. By the end, they should emerge as fuller versions of themselves, transformed by the experiences and choices they've made.

Growth and development throughout the story are essential to keep readers engaged and invested in your characters. Consider the transformation of Feyre in "A Court of Thorns and Roses", where she evolves from a survivor driven by necessity to a powerful being in control of her own destiny. Encourage your characters to make tough decisions, the outcomes of which should challenge them and force growth. Their development should be woven into both the romance and the paranormal plot, each aspect helping to drive the other. As they encounter each new supernatural twist or romantic turn, ensure that it tests their limits and broadens their horizons. And always show, rather than tell, this growth through actions, dialogue, and reactions that align with the increasing complexities they face.

Characters change and evolve not just through their triumphs, but also through their failures and fears. In "Dead Until Dark", Sookie Stackhouse's resilience is shaped as much by her vulnerabilities as by her courage in facing the supernatural world. Don't be afraid to let your characters stumble or take missteps—these moments are powerful catalysts for development. As they grapple with their paranormal reality and romantic entanglements, allow their failures to be as formative as their victories. These setbacks contribute to a more relatable and compelling arc, deepening the readers' connection to the characters. Their evolution, by the end, should be a tapestry of their experiences, both good and bad, that makes their final triumph all the more satisfying.

The heart of character development lies in the choices your characters make. In "The Vampire Academy" series, Rose Hathaway's journey is marked by her decisions, often between her own desires and her duty. Give your characters difficult choices that reflect the internal conflict between what they want and what they need. As they navigate a world where the paranormal intertwines with the mundane, these choices should come with high stakes and lasting consequences. Their decisions should not only advance the plot but also reflect their growing complexity as characters, continuously shaping their paths. As their creator, you must be brave enough to let them make the wrong choices sometimes, as these are often the moments that catalyze the greatest growth.

Integration of a character's backstory is vital for understanding their motives and reactions within the paranormal realm. In "The Witching Hour" by Anne Rice, the Mayfair witches' history shapes their identities and influences their romantic destinies. Weave in your characters' histories gradually, allowing readers to uncover the reasons behind their fears, hopes, and desires as the story unfolds. Their past should serve as a foundation for their development, informing their decisions and their evolution in the face of paranormal events. Think of backstory as the undercurrent that propels your characters forward, driving the transformation that occurs within them as they confront each new supernatural or romantic challenge.

A fundamental aspect of character evolution is how they handle relationships beyond the romantic lead. Look at how Katniss Everdeen's connections with others in "The Hunger Games" affect her growth throughout the series. Each relationship, whether it's with a friend, family member, or rival, should push your characters to evolve, often in ways they do not anticipate. Their interactions with side characters can mirror their inner journey, providing a multi-dimensional view of their growth. Ensure that these relationships have depth and impact, influencing the protagonists in both the paranormal and romantic threads of your story. Through the lens of these other relationships, readers can witness a broader range of the characters' emotions and growth.

To spark evolution in your characters, introduce elements of self-reflection within the paranormal context. In "City of Bones", Clary Fray's discovery of the Shadowhunter world forces her to reconsider her identity and her place in the world. Supply moments where your characters ponder their place within the supernatural community and their romantic entanglements, prompting internal change. These reflective moments should be catalysts for transformation, illuminating the characters' paths towards self-discovery and evolution. As they come to grips with their paranormal existence and its implications for their relationship, their inner growth should be clear and resonate with the reader. It's these revelations that often lead to the most compelling and satisfying character arcs.

Moreover, ensure that your characters' evolution is believable within the world rules you've created. In "The Southern Vampire Mysteries", Sookie's growth parallels her increasing understanding of and engagement with the supernatural world around her. Her abilities and the choices she makes are grounded in the reality of the series, lending credibility to her development. As your characters change, their transformations must make sense within the context of the paranormal elements you've established. This internal consistency is what allows readers to suspend disbelief and fully invest in the characters' journeys.

The evolution of your paranormal romance characters should be mirrored by their increasing power or understanding of the supernatural elements they're dealing with. Hermione Granger's journey in "Harry Potter" showcases how her mastery of magic grew hand-in-hand with her personal growth. Whether they begin the story with powers or acquire them along the way, the development of these abilities should reflect and enhance their character arc. The romantic thread can also be interwoven here, with the characters' supernatural growth either aiding or complicating their relationships. Balancing these aspects thoughtfully can lead to characters that are not only powerful in their own right but also compelling in their complexity and relatability.

Evolution also comes from testing your characters' beliefs and values. In "The Bone Season" series, Paige's worldview is constantly challenged, reshaping her character with each new revelation. Place your characters in situations where their morals are questioned, their loyalties are tested, and their beliefs are turned upside down. This is especially intriguing in the context of a paranormal world where the usual rules may not apply. Their ideals and their romantic inclinations should clash with the realities they face, compelling them to evolve or reevaluate their stance. These moral dilemmas anchor character development in emotional truths, making their journey towards or away from change deeply personal.

Embrace the possibility of love as a transformative power in your characters' development. Just as Lestat's relationship with Louis alters his trajectory in "The Vampire Chronicles", so too should your characters be changed by their romances. Love, especially in a paranormal setting, can act as a catalyst for self-discovery and character evolution. It often forces characters to confront aspects of themselves they've ignored or suppressed. While the love story should not be the sole factor for change, it should be a significant one, dubbed seamlessly into the fabric of the characters' arc. The strength and depth of their love should reflect and propel their personal growth, making it an integral part of their evolving identity.

Characters should also evolve through their alliances and enmities within the paranormal landscape. Take inspiration from "The Dresden Files" where Harry Dresden's relations with various supernatural entities affect his development. These alliances and rivalries can test the characters' resolve, adaptability, and morality, charting a course for growth. The dynamics of these relationships can both mirror and complicate their romantic storylines, adding layers to both plots and character arcs. How they navigate these treacherous waters, whom they choose to trust or fight, will define their journey and flesh out their evolution, adding shades of complexity to their character.

Furthermore, don't shy away from letting your characters backslide occasionally. Just as Roland in Stephen King's "The Dark Tower" series experiences setbacks in his quest, so should your characters experience reversals in their growth. These moments can feel disappointing, but they're also profoundly human, providing depth and realism to your character's arc. The key is to ensure that each backslide is a moment of learning and adds to the character's trajectory towards change. Their missteps should be as instructive as their successes, maybe even more so because it is often our failures that teach us the most.

Lastly, consider the end goal of your characters' evolution. As with any good story, there should be a sense of closure or, at the very least, a significant realization—an "aha!" moment much like the enlightenment Rhysand and Feyre reach in "A Court of Mist and Fury". Even if the story continues beyond the current book, the characters should reach a pivotal point of growth by the end of each installment. Give your readers a clear sense of how far the characters have come, but also leave them with questions: How will this change last? What new challenges will this evolution bring? Leave room for further growth, setting the stage for an even more intricate and satisfying arc in the next adventure.

Chapter 14

Supporting Cast

Supporting characters in your paranormal romance aren't just the backdrop for your main characters; they are the vibrant colors adding depth and texture to your canvas. Think of the rich assortment of friends and foes in "The All Souls Trilogy", each with their own agendas and personalities that enrich the tapestry of the story. These characters should each have their own distinct voice, goals, and arcs that intersect with, but don't overshadow, the main romance. They provide relief, insight, and often a mirror to reflect the growth of your protagonists. Make sure they serve a purpose in driving the plot forward, whether as allies, antagonists, or simply as foils to your protagonists. Each should feel like a main character in their own right, living a story that happens to cross paths with your central romance.

The importance of side characters cannot be overstated—they often hold the keys to the subplots that make your world feel real. In "The Vampire Chronicles", Anne Rice creates a full-blooded cast, each capable of starring in their own tale. They add layers to your narrative, influencing the protagonists and providing alternative viewpoints on the world you've crafted. Through their eyes, readers can explore the corners of your paranormal universe that lie beyond the direct vision of your main characters. They also serve as vital tools to pace your main narrative; use them to slow things down, provide necessary exposition, or ramp up the tension. They should fulfill roles that bolster the main story, without which the narrative would feel incomplete or less vibrant.

Making your supporting characters memorable is critical to your story's resonance. Think about how Zuzana in "Daughter of Smoke and Bone" stands out with her quirky personality and steadfast loyalty. You want your readers to be able to recall them with clarity, whether it's through a unique physical trait, a relentless inner motivation, or a way of speaking that sets them apart. They should be crafted with as much care as your main characters, avoiding stereotypes in favor of complexities and contradictions that evoke real people. These characters provide richness to the world you've built and offer readers multiple figures to cheer for, cry over, and, sometimes, love to hate. Ensure they each get their moment to shine, allowing the readers an opportunity to forge an emotional connection.

One key to creating supporting characters who are memorable and supportive is to intertwine their stories with the central romance without overshadowing it. In "A Discovery of Witches", secondary characters like vampire Marcus and witch Sophie play crucial roles yet their stories complement rather than compete with the protagonists'. They may carry their own desires and narrative weight, but these subplots enhance the main romance, illustrating various aspects of love or providing contrasts to the core relationship. Strong supporting characters can also serve as sounding boards or advisors to the protagonists, nudging them in the right direction or offering a different perspective on their supernatural situation. Their interactions with the main couple are opportunities to develop the central theme and deepen the emotional stakes.

Supporting characters can also ground your paranormal romance in reality, offering a touchstone to the familiar in a world of the fantastic. Jacob Black from "Twilight" starts as a connection to the human side of Bella's life before his own supernatural nature emerges. They create a sense of normalcy or a reference point for readers, anchoring the extraordinary elements of your story with the relatability of everyday life. While they may become swept up in the paranormal, their reactions and interactions with these elements can serve to make readers feel more at home in your story's fantastical world. They can add an element of the mundane amidst the magic and monsters, serving as a valuable thread linking the reader's understanding with the unfolding narrative.

Moreover, think about how each supporting character expands the world of your paranormal romance. For instance, the Night Court's inner circle in "A Court of Mist and Fury" each reveal different facets of the faerie realm and its politics. These characters allow you to flesh out the complexities of your world, offering different perspectives and experiences that your main couple might never encounter. They each carry a piece of the world's puzzle, offering information and insights that enrich the readers' understanding and investment in your story's universe. Furthermore, their diversity of beliefs and backgrounds can add layers of conflict and cooperation that both test and bolster the romance at your novel's heart.

Remember that each supporting character has the potential for growth and development just like your protagonists. The swordsman Inigo Montoya in "The Princess Bride" embarks on a journey as compelling as that of Buttercup and Westley, complete with his own goals and character arc. These secondary figures should evolve, confront their own challenges, and overcome obstacles, which in turn affects the main storyline. Their arcs provide additional emotional investment for the readers and can parallel or contrast with the primary romance, highlighting themes of love, sacrifice, and transformation within the broader narrative. Craft these characters with intention, knowing that their development can weave additional richness into the fabric of your story.

Supporting characters also have the distinct role of reflecting the inner turmoil or joy of the main characters. In "The Iron Fey" series, Puck plays off the protagonist Meghan's emotions, amplifying the dramatic tension and offering levity or insight when needed. Use your side characters as foils or mirrors, their experiences and reactions help to reinforce or question the choices of your main couple. They can bring out sides of your primary characters you want to explore, serving as catalysts for their transformation. Through their actions and their relationship to the main couple, these secondary characters can bring clarity to complex emotional landscapes or underscore the story's deeper messages.

Moreover, some of the best supporting characters illuminate aspects of the paranormal world that your main characters might not be privy to. In "The Raven Boys", each member of Blue's household offers a unique slice of the clairvoyant community, enriching the story's magical aspects. These characters can guide your protagonists—and your readers—deeper into the lore and laws of your created world. They might carry wisdom or warnings that your main couple needs to heed, and in that capacity, they become invaluable to the overarching narrative. Make sure each of them feels necessary, their presence not just as character dressing, but integral to the unfolding of your paranormal tale.

Furthermore, your side characters can serve as the emotional heartbeat of the story. Simon in "The Mortal Instruments" is a linchpin for many emotional moments, balancing out the supernatural with his human reactions. They often provide support to the protagonist, offering a shoulder to cry on or a congratulatory cheer. They can also be the source of necessary conflict, challenging and prodding your main characters in ways that test and ultimately strengthen them. Through their agency, the emotional stakes are raised, as the reader comes to care not just for the outcome of the central romance, but for the fates of these critical secondary figures as well.

Balancing a diverse ensemble cast means ensuring none of your supporting characters become mere plot devices. Much like Bonnie Bennett in "The Vampire Diaries", who grows from a friend with useful witch powers to a well-rounded character with her own significant storyline, each character should have moments of independence from the main romance. It's important for side characters to have agency—to make choices that affect the story in their own right, not just when it's convenient for the main plot. This creates a more believable world and maintains the immersion necessary to keep readers invested from cover to cover. Crafting real stakes for these secondary characters is key to making them memorable and essential, not just to the story but to the readers' experience.

In addition, the best side characters can surprise your reader and even you as the author. Think about how Captain Thorne in "The Lunar Chronicles" often steals the scene with his unpredictability and charisma. Allow your supporting cast the freedom to take the story in unexpected directions, creating moments of delight or tension that you hadn't initially planned. These spontaneous shifts can enrich the narrative, opening up new plot lines or emotional depths within the main romance. Embracing uncertainty within your side characters can lead to a more dynamic and engaging story overall.

Some of the most memorable supporting characters in paranormal romance are those that embody qualities or experiences that contrast with the supernatural elements at play. This can be seen in figures like Leslie in "Wicked Lovely", who represents the mortal world's stark realism amid the story's faerie enchantments. These characters can challenge or reinforce the bizarre and wonderful aspects of your paranormal world, creating a back-and-forth dialogue between the ordinary and the extraordinary. They ground the narrative, reminding readers of what is at stake in the human world even as your characters delve deeper into the supernatural romance.

Finally, consider the longevity of your supporting characters in the context of your series potential. Magnus Bane in "The Mortal Instruments" series provided not just vital support across the saga but also enough intrigue to eventually helm his own stories. Plan for characters that could potentially spin off into their own tales, or who offer enough intrigue and mysterious backstories to pique ongoing reader interest. Your supporting cast should have staying power, maintaining relevancy from book one to book ten, equipped with the substance to potentially last beyond the confines of a single story.

Remember, creating a rich supporting cast takes as much care as crafting your main characters. These characters can become beloved friends to your readers, and their stories and development are crucial to building an engaging, immersive world that fans will want to return to time and again.

Chapter 15

Setting Descriptions

When describing your setting, begin with the most striking feature that captures the essence of the place. If your paranormal romance unfolds in a gothic mansion like in "Blackwood Farm", its looming presence should cast an omnipresent shadow over the narrative. Start with the towering spires that pierce the sky, the way the ivy clings to the stone like a persistent memory, or the gargoyles that smirk from their perches. Use rich adjectives sparingly, allowing the natural intrigue of the setting to stand on its own. Show how the light filters through the stained-glass windows, casting colorful patterns across the cobweb-laden foyer. Ground your readers with a strong visual before you plunge them into the shadows of the unknown.

Making your paranormal world come alive means engaging beyond the visual. Consider the jarring harmony of the singing sands in "The Star-Touched Queen", which bring with them tales of wonder and woe. Bring in the whispers of the wind as it shares ancient secrets with those who would listen. Describe how the earth pulses with a heartbeat, a rhythm that promises magic and mystery. Let the trees in your haunted forest hiss with the wisdom of centuries, bending to guide or to threaten. Root your readers into the landscape with descriptors that suggest life and movement, an environment that is an active participant in its own story.

To describe your settings vividly, use all senses. Let the atmosphere envelop your reader as it does your characters. Imagine stepping into the Belle Époque Paris of "The Beautiful". The air would be dense with the mingling scents of perfumes and pastries, overlaid with the subtle undercurrent of something ancient and primal hiding just beneath the surface. Your characters might hear the distant echo of laughter from cabarets, the soft rustle of silk gowns whisking through cobbled streets, and under it all, the night whispers of creatures best left unnamed. Engaging all senses creates a fully fleshed out world, one that feels real enough to step into.

To truly make your setting breathe, consider the tactical sensations that your environment evokes. The oppressive humidity of New Orleans in "The Casquette Girls" clings to the skin like a second layer, as if the city itself wants to get closer to those who dare walk its haunted streets. Let your reader feel the rough bark of a tree where fairies nest, the cool, smooth surface of an ancient altar, the sharp sting of a thorn in a bewitched rose garden. Touch grounds your reader, pulling them into the tangibility of your paranormal world. It's these details that lend authenticity and vitality to the realm you've created.

Dive deeper into the textures of your world by describing the specific and varied scents that might be present in a particular setting. As seen in "Serpent & Dove", the witch's lair is ripe with the heady aroma of herbs, the musty tang of old books, and the faint, lingering scent of magic that prickles at the senses. Incorporate the smell of rain on cobbled streets, the burn of silver to a werewolf's nose, or the intoxicating fragrance of a flower only found on the cusp of the otherworld. Scent is one of the most powerful memory triggers, and by borrowing this in your descriptions, you create an experience that sticks to the readers long after they close the book.

The taste of the air in a place can also tell a story of its own. Perhaps in your world, the closer one gets to the hidden world of the Fae, the more the air tastes like honey or, conversely, like ash as one approaches a vampire's underground lair. This feature in "The Cruel Prince" subtly indicates a trespass into otherworldly territory. Let your character's environment change not only with sights and sounds but with the way the air sits heavy on their tongue, or how each breath carries the bitter hint of dark magic at work. It's an oft-neglected sense in writing but can be one of the most immersive when used well.

Sound is a dynamic tool to make your setting stand out. In "The Raven Boys", the buzzing energy of a ley line is almost a character in itself, a sound that gets under the skin. Let your readers hear the crackling of a witch's spell, the distant howl of a wolf that sets local dogs into a frenzy, or the eerie silence of a ghost town. Use sound to build atmosphere; let the drip of a mysterious liquid or the rustle of leaves in a place devoid of wind add an edge of tension to your prose. The sounds your characters hear can act as foreshadowing and help build suspense, holding your readers' nerves taut as they read.

Remember to craft each setting description with purpose, moving the story or the development of your characters forward. As with the bone-littered caves that serve as both setting and symbol of the protagonist's fears in "City of Ghosts", the environment can reflect internal struggles. Use your settings to enhance the emotions of a scene; the claustrophobic heat of a vampire's lair can amplify the intensity of a confrontation, while the liberating vastness of an open field under the full moon can mirror a character's sense of newfound freedom. The places your characters occupy should never be incidental; they should be an essential piece of the storytelling.

Weather and time of day can dramatically affect the ambiance in your setting. The velvet cloak of night in "Nightshade" wraps around the characters, shrouding their actions in secrecy and danger. Describe how the moonlight filters through twisted branches, or how the early morning fog chills to the bone and clouds vision, laying a blanket of mystery over a scene. Sunlight, or its absence, can transform a benign location into something foreboding, and a well-timed thunderstorm can heighten drama in an instant. Use these elements to underscore the mood you wish to set —weather and time can be your allies in painting a vivid scene.

When painting a scene, be specific but also leave room for the reader's imagination to fill in some blanks. Sometimes, a hint of movement at the corner of a character's eye in "The Diviners" is more suspenseful than a detailed description of the creature lurking there. Use ambiguities to your advantage, employing suggestive phrases that stoke the imagination. By not stating everything explicitly, you create an interactive experience that invites readers to build their own fears or wonders into the setting, making it their own unique version of haunting or miraculous.

To depict a unique location, consider mixing the ordinary with the extraordinary. Show how a normal metropolitan city teems with unseen magic—a subway where spells are bartered or a park where goblins gather after dark like in

"The Enchantment Emporium". Highlight the small irregularities that indicate the existence of magic; the door that leads to an otherworldly diner or the mirror that doesn't quite reflect what's in front of it. These details make your setting pop with the unexpected and the uncanny, giving it a flavor that stays with the reader.

Consider, too, the history embedded within your settings. The dilapidated ruins of a once grand witch's enclave in "The Witchlands" speak of better times, of power now waned. Describe the faded grandeur of such a place, the old enchantments clinging to the crumbling walls, the whispers of past glory heard through the sighing winds. Let the decay tell its tale, and in doing so, reveal more about the world your characters inhabit. History can be a character in itself, lending gravitas and a sense of the epic to the story you weave.

In the echo of chambers in abandoned catacombs or the hollows of an ancient tree, consider the silence within your setting. Silence can be as telling as sound. In "Shadow and Bone", the protagonist's hushed awe when encountering the Shadow Fold lends to the creation of the world as much as any spoken dialogue. Silent moments can be pregnant with tension, expectation, or awe. Use the absence of sound to create a canvas upon which readers can project their anticipation or fear. Silence can be as rich a tool as any lush description.

Lastly, the contrasts within your setting can help deepen the world's dimensions. A garden that blooms in the heart of a dark, enchanted forest in "The Iron King" can be a respite for characters and readers alike. Play with light and shadow, moments of beauty in the midst of danger, or pockets of warmth in the cold. This juxtaposition not only creates visual interest but also reinforces the themes of your story. The fleeting beauty amongst the dark can symbolize hope, the promise of love, or a brief respite in a character's troubled journey. It's these contrasts that make your settings memorable and provide them with an emotional resonance that complements your narrative.

Describing your setting isn't just about painting a scene; it's about creating an experience. It should be as alive and as changeable as your characters, influencing and defining them just as they are shaped and confined by it. By using all senses to describe your settings, you bring readers into a tangible world that they can almost touch, smell, and taste, fully immersing them in the paranormal romance you've crafted. Each scene should entice the reader to delve deeper, explore further, and lose themselves completely in the world you've woven from shadows and whispers, longing and mystery.

Chapter 16

Incorporating History & Lore

Incorporating history and lore into your paranormal romance offers a profound depth that can elevate your narrative. Consider the layered histories that enrich "Jonathan Strange & Mr Norrell", setting a stage where magic feels rooted in the British Isles. When you thread history into your story, you forge a connection that grounds your paranormal events in reality. Research historical events that resonate with the supernatural elements you wish to explore and think about how they might have played out unseen. Perhaps your witches influenced the outcome of battles, or your shapeshifters migrated across continents, hidden within major population movements. Use these threads to create a tapestry that intertwines the factual and the fantastical, lending credibility and texture to your novel's backdrop.

Using myths and legends is like inviting timeless story-tellers into your narrative. Make your romance reverberate with the echoes of stories like "The Golem and the Jinni", where ancient tales merge seamlessly with the protagonists' arc. Delve into folklore to find creatures and tales that you can reinterpret and weave into your story's fabric. Whether you draw on well-known epics or obscure myths, ensure that they are adapted to serve your plot and support your characters' journeys. Consider how these legendary beings and events might be interpreted through modern eyes, and use them to shed light on your characters' experiences. Remember that myths and legends come from a kernel of truth—let that truth inform the authenticity of your paranormal world.

Creating your own backstory delivers a world that is uniquely yours. When you tread the untouched snow of lore as "Mistborn" does, your narrative carries the weight of originality. Craft a history that speaks to the powers, creatures, and societies of your world. These backstories should be rich with conflict, triumphs, and mysteries that have shaped the current landscape in which your characters reside. Bear in mind that like an iceberg, much of a backstory will exist below the surface, unseen but vital to the structure of the world it supports. Always keep your lore consistent and refer back to it as a touchstone as your characters navigate their arcs against this rich historical canvas.

Consider how cultural history can influence the paranormal aspects of your world, much like "The City of Brass" draws from Middle Eastern history and lore. Perhaps the traditions and rituals of your world's inhabitants stem from historical events or ancient beliefs that still hold sway. These cultural footprints can help shape societal structures, inform conflicts, and enrich your setting. The legacies of the past should ripple through your characters' lives, influencing their worldviews and prejudices. This reflection of history can empower your characters to struggle against or embrace their heritage, adding further dimension to their personal growth.

When building your lore, ensure it drives the story rather than simply decorating it. In "The Lions of Al-Rassan", the history of a fantasy land inspired by medieval Spain is integrally woven into every motive and mission. Shape your backstory such that it has a direct impact on your characters' present lives—the curse they're trying to break, the legacy they're striving to uphold, or the history they're attempting to either repeat or avoid. The historical layers you create should be more than a mere backdrop; they must be the catalyst for action, the puzzle to be solved, and the heritage that defines identities.

Use historical conflicts as a basis for the tensions within your paranormal world, in the vein of "Under Heaven", where dynamism of Tang Dynasty politics offers a captivating mirror. Just as political strife and social upheaval have been constants throughout history, they can act as undercurrents in your narrative, providing a believable context for the supernatural elements of your story. Whether it's a war between witch covens mirroring the wars of religion or vampire clans playing roles in political intrigue, these elements can add a familiar layer to the paranormal aspects. Make these historical tensions personal for your characters, with ancestry, ancient grudges, or inherited responsibilities shaping their everyday lives and the choices they make.

History can also serve as a tool for mystery and uncovering truth in your narrative. In "The Infernal Devices", the protagonists unravel secrets engrained in London's steam-punk-esque history. Use hidden history or lore as a quest for your characters, driving the plot forward as they uncover truths about themselves or their world. Consider having historical sites be actual places of power or secret meeting spots for supernatural entities. The uncovering of history then becomes an adventure, propelling your char-acters to discover both literal and figurative pieces of a puzzle that once solved, illuminate the broader picture of your story.

Channeling legends offers an opportunity to play with reader expectations. By incorporating a well-known legend like King Arthur's in "The Once and Future King", you tap into a vein of familiarity; you can uphold or subvert these legends to surprise and delight your reader. Offer a twist on a classic tale or character that elicits an "aha!" moment, adding a layer of connectivity between the familiar and the new. This juxtaposition of known and unknown enriches your world, providing fodder for conversation, debate, and reader engagement. Who knows, your twist might become the next iteration of the myth for future generations.

Myths traditionally explain the unexplainable, which can act as a source of conflict or solution in your story's world. Envision how myths in "Tigana" are used as both historical motivation and mystical resolutions. Perhaps a character's ability was once explained through myth, but now they struggle against this preconceived notion. Alternatively, myths might hold answers to secrets your protagonists seek or serve as warnings for the dangers they face. Let the myths in your story live and breathe, becoming an active part of your characters' understanding of their world.

Draw on the power of creation myths to build the foundation of your world's existence, like the detailed beginning of the universe in "The Silmarillion". An origin story can explain why the world functions as it does, providing a rationale for the rules of magic, the presence of supernatural creatures, or the conflicts that prevail. Your creation myth doesn't have to be exhaustive, but it should offer a reference point for the characters and readers alike, as well as a source of ancient wisdom or foreboding prophecies. A strong creation myth can bind your world together, making it cohesive and more immersive.

Reflect on the role of artifacts and ancient objects within your narrative, as with "The Amulet of Samarkand". Artifacts can be imbued with historical significance and power, becoming central to the plot or character development. They can also be a tangible link to the past, holding secrets or memories that are vital to understanding the current conflict. This can create a direct connection between your characters and the bygone events shaping their lives, revealing backstory in a way that is engaging and interactive. Let these artifacts carry the weight of history, and let their revelation be a touchstone that reveals the depth of your world.

Leveraging real historical figures as characters or reference points for lore can lend credibility to your story, like it does in "Outlander" with its cast from the Jacobite risings. Consider how you might weave actual personalities into the fabric of your paranormal tale. It could be through a character who once knew Leonardo da Vinci or a secret society that protected the likes of Nostradamus. These figures can add a sense of veracity and intrigue to your story, tying the real with the unfathomable and compelling readers to question what might indeed be possible.

Integrate historical events by showing their impact on the present day, as "The Historian" does with the folklore of Dracula seeping into modern times. Use descriptive flashbacks, found diaries, letters, or secrets passed down through generations. These breadcrumbs of the past should feel like a natural part of the narrative, not forced exposition. They should add urgency or depth to the current events, explaining old feuds, power struggles, or age-old alliances that still affect the world your characters navigate. Let history feel alive and influential, rather than static and distant.

Historical events can serve as an allegory for your current-day story, with your characters living through similar dilemmas or struggles. The Haitian Revolution is mirrored in the tension of the colonial and magical power dynamics in "The Kingdom of This World". Such parallels can lend a sense of timelessness to your narrative, making the case that certain themes are eternal. Readers will be drawn to the semblance between past and present, encouraging them to draw connections and invest deeper in your tale's outcome.

Finally, creating your own backstory will require balance—revealing enough to engage the reader without overwhelming them with exposition. Weave your lore into the dialogue, setting, and internal reflections, as subtly crafted in "Spinning Silver". This information should be disclosed naturally, without stalling the plot or romance. Let the richness of your world unravel as the characters face their challenges, allowing readers to piece together the puzzle alongside them, reveling in each new discovery that brings the past alive. Your backstory should support and enhance your narrative, shining a light on the path your characters are destined to walk.

Chapter 17

Balancing the Ordinary & Extraordinary

Balancing the ordinary and the extraordinary in your paranormal romance is like baking a cake with the right measurements of sugar and spice. You want to entice your readers with the allure of the supernatural, much as "A Discovery of Witches" lures us into a world where ancient manuscripts hold dark secrets. Yet, you also want to ground your story in the realm of the everyday, relatable experiences that anchor your paranormal twists. Your protagonists should live in a world where supernatural occurrences are as real as a morning cup of coffee. To achieve this balance, juxtapose fantastical elements with mundane tasks—perhaps your heroine deciphers an ancient curse while on hold with customer service. Let the spectacular illuminate the ordinary, and have the everyday context give weight to the wonders you create.

Integrating the paranormal into the everyday means turning the mundane world into a place of hidden magic. Consider how "Garden Spells" makes us believe a quaint town garden can influence the lives of its inhabitants. It's about seeing the extraordinary potential in ordinary things: a mirror that shows more than reflections, a storm that whispers secrets, a painting that watches. Let the paranormal elements bleed into the fabric of daily life, so they become as accepted by the reader as they are by your characters. The key to seamless integration is consistency; set the rules for how the supernatural interacts with the mundane and stick to them. Through repetition and detail, what was once extraordinary becomes part of the routine.

Making the paranormal believable for readers is a matter of constructing a solid bridge between reality and fantasy. In the world of "The Raven Boys", the search for an ancient Welsh king exists alongside homework and high school drama. Start by rooting your characters in reality: give them jobs, families, hobbies, flaws, and all the trivial worries of normal life. Then, thread the paranormal through these everyday concerns so that the fantastical elements arise organically. It should feel as if magic has always been a layer beneath the surface of the world, waiting to be brushed away. Your reader's belief hinges on the plausibility and logic you weave into your narrative fabric.

Your characters provide the key to balancing the extraordinary with the ordinary. Like Mercy Thompson in "Moon Called", who is a mechanic as well as a shapeshifter, they should personify this blend. They go to work, pay bills, and fall in love, but they also navigate curses, pack politics, or hidden realms. By grounding your characters in the real world, with tangible concerns and relatable emotions, you make the paranormal aspects of their lives more digestible. Let your readers see themselves in your characters' humanity so that they accept the supernatural attributes as extensions of a reality they recognize. This duality is what makes a paranormal romance relatable and exciting.

To integrate the paranormal naturally, use humor and irony to highlight the clash between the magical and the mundane. "Practical Magic" achieves this by juxtaposing the pressures of a small-town life with the complexities of witchcraft. Perhaps your protagonist is late to a date not because of traffic, but because a potion took too long to brew. Use these contrasts to elicit a chuckle or a nod from your readers, acknowledging the absurdity of the situation. This levity can make the existence of the extraordinary within the everyday more palatable, drawing your readers further into the whimsy and wonder of your world.

Building a world where the extraordinary is a commonplace affair takes careful crafting. The residents of Bon

Temps in "Dead Until Dark" view the supernatural as another piece of their small-town drama. Introduce your paranormal elements gradually—let them simmer beneath the surface before bringing them to a boil. The abnormal should creep into the normal, slowly encroaching upon the world until the reader can no longer pinpoint when the unlikely became the inevitable. As your characters encounter the supernatural, their reactions—from disbelief to acceptance—will mirror and guide your reader's journey.

To create believability within your extraordinary circumstances, allow skepticism to exist within your narrative. Not every character in "Storm Front" readily accepts the world of magic that Dresden inhabits. Bring in doubters and skeptics, and let their doubts reflect those a reader might have. Then, systematically break down those doubts through the plot progression, revealing the paranormal as inescapably real. This measured conversion from skepticism to belief will allow your readers the same gratifying discovery of wonder within the credible world you've built.

Remember that the smallest details can enrich the believability of your paranormal world. In "The Night Huntress" series, the vampire culture is fleshed out with politics and social norms. Imagine what supernatural beings would have in their homes, how they would modify their clothes for wings or tails, or how they might use magic for everyday chores. These tiny touches demonstrate that you've thoroughly contemplated the integration of the paranormal into your world, making the fusion of the extraordinary with the ordinary that much more convincing for your readers.

When casting a spell of believability over your paranormal world, consistency is your incantation. As shown with the intricately built society of Others in "Written in Red", rules must be adhered to. If a vampire can't enter a home uninvited in chapter two, they can't burst through someone's door in chapter ten without a good reason that fits the established logic. These steadfast rules will construct a solid framework within which the magic of your story can unfold. Your readers will appreciate and cling to this structure, using it to ground themselves in the fantastical elements you present.

Occasionally let the extraordinary disrupt the ordinary in a way that shifts the story's course. "The Southern Book Club's Guide to Slaying Vampires" presents the supernatural as a puzzle that impacts the characters' typical suburban life. Picture a routine family dinner interrupted by a ghostly apparition or a school dance thrown into chaos by a sudden spell gone awry. These interruptions offer chances to propel the plot and force character growth within the context of the extraordinary becoming part of the tapestry of daily life.

Make your paranormal elements integral to the development of the romance at the heart of your story. In "The Shape of Water", the bond between Elisa and the Amphibian Man is defined by the extraordinary circumstances they face. Consider how having a relationship with a werewolf might affect how dates are planned, taking the lunar cycle into account. Or imagine how a human would learn to communicate love to a partner who is a telepath—where no thought can truly be private. By interweaving the supernatural with the romantic, the paranormal becomes an indispensable element of the love story, creating a dynamic that feels both impossible and deeply real.

To anchor the grandeur of the supernatural, provide solid motives rooted in everyday desires and fears. In "The Witch's Daughter", the witch's quest for knowledge and survival spans centuries, yet is grounded in relatable human emotions. Your characters may wield immense power or live for eons, but their motivations should be recognizable—they love, they desire, they regret. When their extraordinary abilities are a means to achieve all-too-human ends, readers are more likely to suspend disbelief and invest in the characters' journeys.

Use first-person or close third-person perspectives to further ground the extraordinary in the ordinary. Personal narratives, as used with such emotive power in "The Time Traveler's Wife", allow readers to see the world through the eyes of a character for whom the paranormal is just part of life. Share their thoughts and emotions as they navigate the extraordinary, offering an intimate glimpse into their acceptance of the paranormal. This technique helps readers connect more closely with your characters, regarding the extraordinary as a matter-of-fact aspect of their world, and consequently, your readers' as well.

In melding the paranormal with the everyday, let the setting reflect this duality. "Wicked" uses the city of New Orleans not just as a backdrop, but as a living mix of the exotic and familiar. Let the hidden alleys hold doorways to other worlds, the historic buildings be bastions of ancient powers, and local festivals be opportunities to mingle the extraordinary with the commonplace. However, ensure that these landmarks remain rooted in their geographical and cultural context. This makes the blend of fantasy and reality more tangible, as readers can picture the supernatural happening in a place they could visit or live in.

Maintaining a thread of reality amidst the fantastical can often come down to relationships. As seen in "The Lux Series", connections between characters offer a genuine human experience in the midst of the alien and otherworldly. Family dynamics, friendships, and rivalries can keep your characters grounded, providing a counterbalance to the myriad ways in which the paranormal influences their lives. It's through these human connections that readers find a doorway into accepting the extraordinary—they believe in the love, the hate, the camaraderie, and the conflict, thus they can believe in the magic that surrounds it all.

Chapter 18

Plotting

In constructing your paranormal romance, consider plot structure as the skeleton upon which your story will flesh out. A strong structure is key, often following a three-act framework comprising the beginning, middle, and end. Start with your setup, introducing your characters and the ordinary world they inhabit. Then, progress to the inciting incident—the moment when the ordinary becomes extraordinary, pulling your protagonists into the paranormal world. The middle act should see the stakes rising, with conflicts both romantic and supernatural building to a peak. Finally, culminate in a climax that resolves the central conflicts and transitions into a satisfying resolution that leaves room for further exploration if your story extends into a series.

The beginning of your paranormal story should enchant and ensnare your reader, drawing them into the allure of the world you've created. Introduce your protagonist in their natural setting, then quickly introduce an element of the paranormal—the flash of a shadow, a cryptic message, a power they never knew they had. Balance this with hints of the romantic thread to come, whether it's a significant glance from a stranger or an old love that returns, shrouded in mystery. This beginning sets the tone for the entire novel; it should promise excitement, danger, and the thrill of a forbidden love that defies the boundaries of the natural world. The seeds you plant here will grow throughout the narrative, lacing your plot with the intrigue that keeps pages turning.

As the middle of your story unfolds, this is where your plot thickens, the romance intensifies, and the paranormal elements become unavoidable. Love flourishes under the strain of adversity, whether it's from societal expectations or supernatural forces. Develop your characters' arcs in tandem with their relationship, ensuring each twist and turn in the plot challenges and refines them. Tension should escalate to the point where the outcome seems uncertain, both for the romance and the overarching conflict. Balance the action with moments of quiet reflection or tender intimacy that deepen the connection between your characters and your readers. It's in this crucible of the middle act that the strength of your plot structure is truly tested.

The end of your novel is where all threads should converge and weave together to form a resolution that is both believable and satisfying. After leading your readers through a gauntlet of emotional and supernatural hurdles, offer them respite. The climax should resolve the major conflict, quell the paranormal threat, and solidify the romantic bond that has been building throughout the narrative. Do not shy away from the consequences of the choices your characters have made; let their effects resonate in the ending. But also, infuse your conclusion with hope and the promise of continuity—whether for your characters' love, their personal growth, or the ever-evolving world they inhabit. Leave your readers with a sense of completion, yet a yearning to return to the world you've crafted.

A strong opening in your paranormal romance is like a key, unlocking the door to the otherworldly for your reader. Your first chapter needs to intrigue and pose questions that demand answers. Hit the ground running with a dynamic event, or captivate with a mystery that hints at a deeper lore. It's this initial hook that will persuade your reader to invest in the characters and the world you've woven. Paint your protagonists in broad strokes initially, leaving the finer details to be filled in as their journey unfolds—just ensure that from the outset, they're compelling. The opening should whisper promises of the magic and romance to come, luring your readers into a tale they can't resist.

Remember, your plot structure isn't just a checklist; it's a rhythm that guides the heartbeat of your story. Pace your narrative to ebb and flow, giving readers time to breathe in between the surges of action and romance. Think carefully about when to introduce major revelations and twists—too early and you risk peaking too soon; too late and you may lose the momentum entirely. Your plot points are stepping stones across the river of your story; place them in a way that leads your readers confidently forward, but don't make the steps too predictable. Allow for the occasional leap of faith and moments of uncertainty; this keeps the experience exhilarating for your readers.

Delve into your story's initial setup with an eye towards foreshadowing. Plant seeds that will germinate throughout your narrative, offering subtle hints of the twists and turns to come. In these early pages, lay the groundwork for the internal and external conflicts that will drive your characters' motivations and decisions. Your readers should finish the beginning of your novel with a sense of who your characters are, what they yearn for, and the eerie and enchanting elements they will face. A solid setup provides a firm launching pad for the soaring journey ahead.

The middle of your story is a balancing act, maintaining the tension while continually raising the narrative stakes. Craft this section with care, as this is where some stories risk losing steam. Your characters should face mounting pressure from both the romance and the paranormal elements, driving them together and tearing them apart in equal measure. This is also the perfect opportunity to delve deeper into your world's lore, unveiling the rich tapestry of history and mystery you've created. Keep your middle engaging by introducing new characters, revealing hidden secrets, or escalating the romance in ways that feel organic to the plot.

As you build towards the climax, every subplot and secret should start coalescing. The choices your characters make must carry weight, the consequences of their actions rippling forward to affect the outcome. Your end should feel both surprising and inevitable; readers should feel the satisfaction of an unpredictable yet perfectly fitting resolution. Offer closure to the narrative arcs you've woven and ensure your protagonists come out changed, their evolution evident and their love affirmed. Leave your readers feeling that, despite the odds, the love story was destined—fated by the stars and by the otherworldly forces you've masterfully commanded.

A strong opening often jumps right into action or presents an element of mystery or conflict that will propel the story. It's the smell of burnt sage as your protagonist performs a midnight ritual; it's the sudden chill of a ghost brushing past, or the impossible reflection in a century-old mirror. It sets the stage for the conflict and lays the emotional groundwork for the romance. The opening should promise the reader a journey—a thrilling ride through dark forests and into lovers' embraces. Use vivid descriptors and active verbs to pull the reader into the action with immediacy, ensuring that from the first line, your novel is unputdownable.

As you step into the middle of your story, remember that this is where character development is paramount. Your characters should be deepening, their layers and secrets exposed by the trials they face. This is the heart of your story, pulsing with the lifeblood of conflict and passion. The chemistry between your romantic leads should be tangible, sparking in every shared glance, every fraught conversation. Simultaneously, the paranormal elements should be reaching fever pitch, stretching the believability of the world to its limits without breaking it.

In your story's conclusion, don't forget to resolve the smaller threads alongside the primary plot. Each character's journey should come to an end, even if that end is simply the beginning of another story. Your readers have followed these threads throughout the narrative—they deserve the reward of a neatly tied knot. The resolution of the central romance, the fate of your protagonists, and the final state of the paranormal world should all act as anchors that bring the narrative to a satisfying close.

The importance of a strong opening cannot be overstressed—it's the first taste your reader gets of the world you've created and the characters they will follow. In that initial glimpse, you must convey the tone, style, and pace of your story, establishing expectations and enticing with the promise of more. It's a handshake, an invitation, a whisper urging the reader to step into the fog of your story's unknown. Use this opportunity to ensnare their curiosity, to make them feel something for your characters right from the start. Your opening is a promise, one that you must deliver on throughout the pages that follow.

Throughout your plot structure, strive to keep the pacing tight and the action compelling. This is the rhythm that keeps the narrative dance lively and enthralling. Monitor the tempo of your revelations—too fast, and your readers will be overwhelmed; too slow, and they may lose interest. Each chapter's end should be a minor cliffhanger that compels the reader to start the next. The key to effective pacing is the interplay between action and suspense, with each beat punctuated by emotions that ebb and flow.

When crafting the beginning of your plot, make sure that you're not only introducing characters and setting but also posing questions. Pique the reader's curiosity with enigmatic allies, elusive enemies, or unexplained phenomena. These riddles will tether your audience to the storyline, ensuring they stay engaged as they seek answers. As your characters confront the unknown, so too will your readers, locked in step with the unfolding mystery.

In your middle act, as the puzzle of your story becomes more intricate, ensure that each chapter raises the stakes. New obstacles should emerge, further complicating the tangled web of supernatural intrigue and romantic entanglement. The complexities of your characters and their world must gradually build, layer upon layer, until it seems nearly impossible to unravel. This escalating tension is what will propel your readers through the meat of your story, eager for resolution.

As you approach the climax of your story, ensure that it's a culmination of the risks taken and truths uncovered. It stands as the grand stage where love and horror, beauty and darkness coalesce into the decisive moment that defines your characters' futures. Your climax should feel like a thunderclap — the sky split asunder — leaving its echo in the ensuing resolution. Your readers' hearts should race with your protagonists, as the world tilts on the edge of a knife, ready to fall one way or another.

After the climax, your story's end is a time for reflection as much as celebration. In the quiet after the storm, there's an opportunity for an emotional denouement. Explore the changed landscapes, both internal and external, and show the growth that's occurred. Don't rush these final moments; they are the reader's last impression of the world you've created. Let your end mirror your opening—echo the tones set at the beginning, providing a narrative bookend that satisfies and resonates.

In conclusion, a well-structured plot serves as the backbone of your paranormal romance, supporting and shaping the narrative from the haunting beginning through the transformative middle, and finally, into the cathartic end. Remember that a strong opening acts as the inviting front door to your imaginary world, beckoning readers inside. Balance the narrative that unfolds within, ensuring that your readers remain captivated by the dance of the ordinary with the extraordinary, as you guide them towards a finale that lingers in the heart and mind long after the final page is turned.

Chapter 19

Plot Twists and How to Use Them

Plot twists and surprises are the lifeblood of an engrossing paranormal romance. They are the shadowy corners and sudden revelations that take a reader's breath away. When crafting your narrative twists, think of them as the magic tricks within your magician's sleeve; they must be planned meticulously but appear effortless. Lay down subtle clues that, in hindsight, make the readers slap their foreheads, shocked they didn't connect the dots sooner. Twists should challenge the characters' relationships and test their love, binding them closer or tearing them apart with equal cruelty. Every twist propels your story forward, injecting fresh energy and ensuring that your readers remain hooked.

Adding unexpected elements to your story keeps readers on their toes, eagerly turning the pages. It's not just about startling them, but about weaving in developments that pivot the story in a new direction. Introduce a new character who challenges the protagonist's loyalties or reveal that an ally has been a foe all along. Perhaps a trusted mentor holds a dark secret or a villain shows an unexpected moment of vulnerability that changes everything. Even within the realm of the paranormal, defy the typical conventions. Let a ghost fall in love, a vampire seek redemption, or a werewolf crave the restraints of normalcy.

Keeping your readers guessing is akin to guiding them through a maze; they sense the exit but find their path peppered with surprising turns. Avoid predictability by shifting the usual tropes of your chosen paranormal elements. If vampires usually fall for humans, perhaps this time it's the vampire who's ensnared by a witch's charm. Construct your narrative so that when readers think they've grasped the direction of the romance or the rules of your supernatural world, a wrench is thrown into the works—forcing them to question what they know. The essence of mystery lies in uncertainty, and weaving that into your story keeps the allure alive.

When it comes to plot twists, timing is everything. Deploy them strategically—a twist too early might feel unearned, too late might seem desperate. The best twists come when the emotional stakes are at their highest, when the reader is so invested in your characters' journey that the revelation has maximum impact. Think of a twist as an intense spike in the heartbeat of your narrative—it should jar, invigorate, and provoke a strong response. Whether it's an unforeseen enemy, an unlikely ally, or a deep betrayal, make sure each twist arrives at the moment that best amplifies the story's tension and drama.

Introduce elements that defy expectation—not just in events, but in character development. Have your seemingly fearless protagonist show vulnerability at an unexpected moment. Or reveal a hidden strength in the quiet, bookish character that nobody (including the reader) suspected. It's not just about what happens in the plot, but in the people within it; shocks and surprises that arise from within your characters can be just as compelling as those that come from the plot. These moments of unexpected depth or change will keep the reader deeply engaged with your characters and their fate.

Every good story has a rhythm—a pace and tempo—and plot twists add unexpected beats that intrigue and excite. They are the crescendos in a symphony that make a reader's heart race faster. However, maintain that equilibrium; if every chapter ends with a cliffhanger, they can lose their effectiveness. Space out the surprises so each one can be fully appreciated, allowing your readers time to absorb and speculate. Let anticipation build for what might occur next, and then, when the moment is right, turn their expectations on their head.

Plot twists shouldn't be twists for twist's sake; they must serve the story and the characters' arcs. They should unlock new layers of your characters or illuminate hidden facets of your world. A twist is most satisfying when it answers as many questions as it raises. With each surprising revelation, reinforce the motivations and desires that drive your protagonists and the obstacles they face. Make each surprise a stepping stone in the path of their journey, bringing them closer to or further from their goals.

For a twist to truly resonate, it should tap into the emotional core of the story. The astonishment from the outcome of a lovers' quarrel or the revelation of a character's true lineage can change the emotional landscape. An unexpected declaration of love, a sacrifice no one saw coming, or a betrayal that cuts deeper than a knife—these twists hit hardest when they're rooted deep in the emotional ground of your narrative. Your reader's emotional investment turns every turn of events into a personal experience, heightening the thrill of each twist.

The key to a successful plot twist is the artful sowing of seeds throughout the story. Like laying down a breadcrumb trail that readers follow, not realizing it's leading them to a place they never expected to go. As they piece together the clues, the sudden shift in the plot becomes an 'aha' moment, a crystallization of hints and forewarnings that have been sprinkled along the way. Craft each clue with precision, neither too obscure nor too obvious, guiding your readers down a trail that ends with a revelation that feels both astonishing and inevitable.

The most effective twists expose the multi-layered nature of your characters, both heroes and villains alike. Like an onion being peeled, each twist should reveal a new layer, a facet of character or history not previously seen. A villain could act nobly, a trusted ally could betray, or a protagonist may have to embrace their darkest nature to save the day. By constantly evolving your characters, the reader's understanding of them shifts, recasting past actions and motivations in a new light, and keeping the reader guessing about what might happen next.

In crafting plot surprises, don't neglect the minor characters—their arcs can offer ripe ground for unexpected development. A seemingly inconsequential character might be key to unraveling a mystery, or an underestimated sidekick could deliver the critical blow in a pivotal moment. These moments underscore the interconnectedness of your cast, reinforcing the idea that everyone in your story has a role to play. As in life, so in your narrative: exciting opportunities for surprise can come from any direction, at any time.

One effective tactic for surprises lies in defying genre expectations. If the tropes of paranormal romance lead down a well-trodden path, find a side road that offers a new viewpoint. Perhaps the love interest is not the brooding vampire but rather the decisive human who takes matters into their own hands. Maybe the curse believed to spell doom is actually a gift in disguise. By adding a layer of complexity to typical genre scenarios, you craft a story that stands out as fresh

Chapter 20

Resolution

The resolution of your story is where the chaos of conflict, the turbulence of supernatural elements, and the fever of romantic entanglement settle into harmony. It's essential that your readers leave the story with a sense of closure, an exhale after the intense climb of your narrative's action and emotion. This doesn't mean every question must have an answer—in fact, a hint of mystery can spur readers' imaginations and maintain the allure of your world. Your resolution should reflect the journey that the characters and readers have been on, echoing the themes and emotions of the story. It's the bow atop your literary package, tied neatly around the experiences within. Make your resolution cathartic, a destination worthy of the journey, yet leave an open window to the breeze of possibility.

Tying up loose ends in your narrative doesn't just provide clarity—it grants a satisfaction that enhances the overall enjoyment of the story. Throughout your tale, you've spun numerous threads—subplots involving secondary characters, lingering mysteries, promises of revelation. Methodically weave these threads together in a way that makes sense—ensure that each subplot resolution reflects the story's broader themes and contributes to character development. Some revelations might be stunning in their simplicity, while others may be quietly profound, but all should serve to underscore the interconnectedness of your narrative's tapestry. This attention to detail rewards your readers' investment and leaves them feeling gratified with the completeness of your tale.

A satisfying conclusion to a paranormal romance isn't just about a 'happily ever after' for your main characters. It encompasses the feeling that the supernatural elements have been respected, that the rules of your world have held firm, and the character growth feels earned and complete. A good ending circles back to the emotional and thematic starting points of your story, showing growth and change. It demonstrates a resolution not just of plot, but of character —a resolution that leaves your readers with a resonant emotional message. Your ending should inspire contentment, while still leaving an echo of the excitement that pulsed through your book—an emotional souvenir that might tempt your readers to revisit your story again.

To pen a finale that resonates, consider the promises you've made to your readers from the very start. You've set expectations with your opening chapters, teased potential outcomes through the flicker of glances and the thrum of danger. Now it's time to fulfill those promises, ensuring that the risks taken, the loves kindled, and the mysteries proposed all reach their logical and satisfying ends. Wrap up romantic arcs with moments that symbolize the couple's journey and growth. Confirm that your supernatural elements find a resting point, whether it's the sealing of a portal or the culmination of a prophetic vision. Your resolution prevails as the final word on the world you've woven, so make it a powerful affirmation of the narrative journey.

Resolution doesn't mean that every facet of your story's world is uncovered and explained. It's about reaching a natural pause in the lives of your characters—a moment of calm in the eye of the storm. The world you've crafted can continue beyond the pages of this tale, leaving some elements in the periphery for the reader's imagination or potential sequels. Yet for the arc your readers have followed, bring peace, bring answers, and most importantly, bring a sense that regardless of what lies beyond the last page, the story they've invested in is complete.

Tying up loose ends should also involve the secondary characters that have become dear to your readers. These characters have played their parts in the drama and also deserve their resolutions. Whether it's a sidekick finding their bravery, an antagonist receiving their comeuppance, or a mentor witnessing the fruition of their guidance, these resolutions enrich the main narrative. They add layers of satisfaction, ensuring that the world feels fully realized, and no character's journey is left hanging in the narrative ether.

When it comes to a satisfying conclusion, sometimes it is the nuances that matter most. A quiet moment of intimacy between your lovers may leave a deeper impression than the grandest gesture. It's about the weight of everything unsaid finally coming to rest, the shared glances that now hold volumes, the simplest touch imbued with the journey just traversed. Let the profound be found in the moments of quietude, making sure the echoes of their trials and triumphs are felt in even the softest whisper of resolution.

Closing your story is like the final notes in a symphony, they should resonate and linger. Even if your characters will return in sequels, this ending must have a self-contained significance. It's a musical pause, a narrative breath that holds all the notes that came before it—hold it too short, and the story feels rushed; draw it out too long, and the impact diminishes. Strike that perfect chord, and your story will sing in the memory, encasing your reader in the aftershock of completion and fulfillment.

A resolution can act as a mirror, reflecting back the beginning of your story but shown through the scarred and strengthened characters who have survived their journey. The site of their initial fateful encounter, the theme of their first conversation, or the echoes of their opening thoughts—their revisitation reaches deeper meaning as your book draws to a close. The cyclical return to these moments brings your characters' evolution into sharp relief, showing not just where they've been, but who they've chosen to become.

Think of tying up loose ends as solving the final piece of a puzzle. The satisfaction comes from seeing the whole picture come together, a story that once felt fragmented now unified. Secondary plots should interlock with the main narrative, solving or dissolving until there's a sense of wholeness. Use the closing chapters to address dangling mysteries, resolve character conflicts, and validate the transformations that have occurred. Taking care of these strands reassures your readers that you've been in control all along, a story-weaver with a master plan.

A satisfying conclusion often revolves around the protagonists' internal journeys as much as their external circumstances. The enemies might have been defeated, and the curses broken, but ensure the growth and struggles of your characters culminate in personal victories too. Perhaps it's self-acceptance in the face of the extraordinary, or love found amidst the chaos—a psychic's peace with their visions, a vampire's acceptance of their nature. It's these personal resolutions that often resonate most deeply with readers, emblematic of the story's impact.

Even the best resolutions must leave a trace of hunger, a desire for just a bit more. You may close the door on this particular narrative, but leave a window cracked open to the possibilities of new adventures or lingering questions. Though you've guided them to a signpost that reads 'The End,' allow your readers to sit and wonder, 'What if?' or 'What next?'. This doesn't mean leaving essential questions unanswered, but rather providing readers with the satisfaction that while this journey is complete, the road continues beyond the horizon—and they are welcome to imagine its path in their minds.

In every resolution, strive for an emotional depth that matches the intensity of the climax. Provide moments of reflection where readers can see the growth achieved, the wounds healed, or the love solidified. A captivating paranormal romance isn't just about resolving the fantastic elements, but also about leaving a lingering emotion with the reader—an ache, a joy, a peace found only through the trials endured by the characters they've grown to love.

Tying up loose ends rewards your reader and your characters. It provides a sense of fulfillment for having journeyed through your world, having experienced its threats and wonders, its love, and losses. Address the lingering subplots that added richness to the main narrative, but ensure they don't overshadow the main story's conclusion. Each loose end tied is a note in the symphony's finale, contributing to the overall harmony, making the music of your story resonate long after the last note has been played.

Ultimately, the conclusion is the last memory readers will carry with them—it's essential that it echoes with satisfaction. A well-crafted ending is a whisper that can roar in reminiscence, and it's your gift to the reader for accompanying you on this spectral journey of the heart. Ensure that when your readers close the book, they do so with reluctance, savoring the taste of the world, the sting of the final battles, and the warmth of resolved romance, carrying with them the promise of your story's spirit and the hope of more to come.

Chapter 21

Leave Readers Hooked

Building suspense in a paranormal romance is akin to drawing back a curtain on a scene that should not be witnessed yet cannot be ignored. Begin by crafting an atmosphere of uncertainty through subtle, strange occurrences that hint at a greater hidden danger. Perhaps your protagonist catches fleeting shadows from the corner of her eye or overhears whispers that seem not quite human. The key is to infuse everyday scenes with a sense of the uncanny, gradually tightening the sense of unease until the reader is on edge, knowing something is amiss but not quite sure what. As the stakes rise with each chapter, layer in the romantic tension, intertwining it with the growing paranormal threat. Let the readers feel the protagonist's fear and curiosity grow in tandem, compelling them to turn the page.

Techniques for keeping readers hooked are multifaceted, utilizing the rich tapestry of plot, character, and setting. Introduce a ticking clock element—perhaps a prophecy that foretells a looming disastrous event, or a curse that must be broken by the full moon. Implement chapter cliffhangers that leave the reader with burning questions, be it an unexpected character's arrival, a sudden disappearance, or a cryptic message. Weave complexities into your characters' backgrounds which suggest they are not all they seem to be. Employ rich descriptions for your paranormal world that make the readers want to linger, even as they feel the chill of foreboding. Most importantly, manage the rhythm of your storytelling; slow down to deepen the intrigue, then accelerate to maintain the momentum.

Gradual reveals and foreshadowing are the breadcrumbs you leave on the path of your narrative. They are promises to your reader that the mysteries you have introduced will have satisfying conclusions. Drop hints about your characters' secret pasts, the true nature of the supernatural elements, or the depths of the romance. Foreshadowing must be subtle—a whispered premonition here, a historical legend recounted there, all building towards revelations that feel earned. With each reveal, the suspense mounts as the pieces of the puzzle start to form a coherent picture, and the reader gets a glimpse of the looming climax. Use these techniques to lay the groundwork for twists that feel surprising yet inevitable, reinforcing your reader's engagement with your story.

Remember that suspense thrives on the unknown, on the reader's anticipation of what might happen next. Craft scenes that make the heart race by placing characters in peril, especially when it's unclear if they'll escape unscathed. But it's not just physical danger that builds suspense; emotional stakes can be just as compelling. A character's inner turmoil over a burgeoning yet potentially doomed romance can simmer with tension. Decisions fraught with supernatural implications can keep your readers questioning and fearful for the outcome. Balance these elements, constantly manipulating the reader's expectations and anxieties to drive the story forward.

One powerful method for keeping readers hooked is the use of prophecies and visions. These can be woven throughout your story, offering both guidance and misdirection. Perhaps your protagonist has been forewarned about the love interest through a cryptic prophecy, infusing their interactions with doubt and suspense. Visions are similarly useful, granting the protagonist—and by extension, the reader—fleeting glimpses of possible futures which may or may not come to pass. Let these prophecies and visions be both a beacon and a maze, illuminating the path even as they confuse it, so that readers are captivated by the puzzle they present.

The mastery of gradual reveals lies in the timing of each disclosure. Unraveling the truth too quickly dissolves tension, while delaying it can breed frustration. Gauge your readers' patience and curiosity, deploying reveals that illuminate the story while spawning new mysteries. Allow these revelations to reshape the relationships within your narrative, especially the romantic arc—perhaps newfound knowledge forces a shift in dynamic or sparks a confrontation laden with emotion. Each reveal should turn the story's wheel, driving your plot and characters into uncharted and always more intriguing territory.

In your hands, foreshadowing is an artful promise of complexity and depth within your story. Hint at your characters' futures through the study of tarot cards, a prophecy uttered in desperation, or omens that hark back to myth and legend. Be sure not to make these hints too blatant; they should feel like pieces of a puzzle that your readers are excited to put together. With foreshadowing, you weave an intricate lace of intrigue, casting shadows that suggest the shape of things to come. Your readers must have faith that you know where each thread leads, trusting you to guide them through the labyrinth you've created.

To build suspense is to play with the reader's mind, teasing them with questions of trust and duplicity. Perhaps your love interest is hiding a paranormal secret too fearful to reveal, or allies are found to be working against the protagonist when the moon rises. Trust is a fragile thing, and as it is tested and broken, suspense twists tighter. Use the characters' web of relationships as a stage for deception and revelation, crafting an experience where not just the plot surprises, but the shifting sands of trust equally captivate. This ebb and flow of trust weaves a compelling narrative fabric, rich with intrigue and steeped in tension.

Varying your pacing is crucial in keeping readers hooked. Not every chapter should end on a high note; allow for moments of calm reflection where the protagonist—and reader—can catch their breath. Though these moments may seem quieter, they can be imbued with their own form of suspense as characters ponder their next move or anticipate a meeting with their beloved. Suspense doesn't always roar; sometimes it whispers, giving readers a chance to muse on the romance's rumbling undercurrents. Let these calm moments not weaken the tension but rather serve as the calm before the storm—a necessary contrast enhancing the impact of the story's more dynamic turns.

Use gradual reveals to show the past intersecting with the present. A character might find an ancestral object connecting them to ancient paranormal events, or unearth a love letter hinting at an affair with implications for their current romantic entanglements. These artifacts from the past serve a dual purpose—deepening the world's lore and teasing out new facets of the narrative yet to be discovered.

With each historical puzzle piece, suspense swells as your readers ponder how history repeats itself or influences the present. Let the characters—and readers—feel the weight of centuries-old secrets as they come to light, heavy with consequence and rich with narrative promise.

Layering your narrative with foreshadowing is like setting a multitude of tiny hooks into your reader's mind, each one tugging them deeper into the story with every chapter. Paint visions of the future in dreams blurred by waking or in the scatter of tarot cards laying out an inscrutable destiny. Let these omens loom in the background, coloring the decisions and emotions of your cast, especially as they navigate the perilous waters of their burgeoning romance. Each chapter's close should feel like the tightening of a noose, the premonition of disaster, or the tension of a cautious hope, keeping your readers bound to the fate of your characters.

Suspense often lies in the whispered possibility of betrayal. Crafting a character who seems allied but whose loyalties remain suspicious can keep readers in a state of delicious doubt. The potential for betrayal becomes a shiver down the spine at each interaction, a question mark lingering over every shared secret. It's the suspicion that makes readers examine every word, every gesture for hidden meanings. Is the romantic lead truly enraptured, or hiding something far more sinister? Play this card close to your chest and reveal the truth with perfect timing, keeping readers ensnared by the thrill of the unknown.

Building suspense is not merely about the events that unfold but the characters who drive them. A protagonist who hesitates at a threshold, torn between the safety of the familiar and the love that calls from beyond, is a wellspring of tension. Craft these internal conflicts with care, as they can be as suspenseful as any external peril. When the stakes are not just the world but the heart, suspense intertwines with emotion, creating a connection that will leave your readers breathless. Let the resonance of the characters' decisions ripple through the paranormal elements of your story, affecting not just their fate but the fabric of the world you've created.

Techniques for keeping readers hooked extend beyond the tangible into the psychological—into the darkest fears and desires of your characters. A confrontation with a supernatural entity can reveal as much about the character as it does the creature. As they face their nightmares, be they literal or figurative, craft these scenes to expose their deepest vulnerabilities, and in doing so, build a suspense that is palpably personal. The fears facing your characters should echo the readers' own, tapping into universal anxieties that claw at the subconscious, urging them to read onwards, seeking closure and relief.

Gradual reveals serve as a crucial technique to maintain the story's enigmatic allure. Consider the slow divulgence of a character's transformation, perhaps a curse that gradually claims them, night by night—the signs subtle at first, but growing more alarming with each chapter. Packaging these developments in layers allows readers to invest not just in the surface narrative, but in the underlying transformation that threads throughout your story. Suspense coiled within the characters' metamorphosis keeps readers on edge, waiting to see the full scope of the supernatural change and its inevitable impact on the romance at the story's core.

Chapter 22

Reader Takeaways

Your reader takeaways are the echoes of the story that linger after the last page has been turned. Beyond the resolution of the central conflict and the culmination of the romance, what remains is the emotional residue—the feelings provoked, the thoughts inspired, and the questions raised. Aim to craft a tale that not only entertains but lingers in the mind and stirs the heart. Your readers should walk away with not only memories of the plot but reflections on the themes—love's resilience, the nature of bravery, or the price of immortality. The best stories are those whose characters become companions long after the final words, whose world continues to unfold in the imagination. Your paranormal romance should aim to be a journey that resonates, leaving trails that readers follow in daydreams and discussions.

What you want readers to remember is akin to a melody that plays on long after the music has stopped. It's the essence of your characters—the strength they found in love, their courage in the face of the paranormal, their growth from within turmoil. Leave markers of poignancy that stand out like beacons—a selfless sacrifice, a moment of profound truth, a choice that was a testament to character. These are the points of impact, the narrative peaks that loom larger than the rest, casting long shadows over the reader's memory. Sculpt these high points with precision, wrapping them in language and emotion that tattoo them onto the heart. In crafting a memorable story, aim for a tapestry of such moments—seared gently onto the soul.

Leaving a lasting impact requires that you invite the reader to form a personal bond with your narrative. Endow your romance with elements that reach beyond the page, tapping into universal experiences and emotions. Perhaps you echo the longing for connection, the terror of the unknown, or the ache for belonging that lies within us all. Weave your narrative so that readers can see a reflection of their lives within the paranormal— uncovering truths about themselves within the escapism. Your story's impact comes from its ability to resonate with personal truth while offering an enticing flight from reality. When the threads of the personal intertwine with the fantasy, the resulting tapestry is one that captures and endures.

Reader takeaways are shaped not only by the narrative but by the thematic subtext that threads through every chapter. Infuse your story with themes that challenge and provoke —the sanctity of trust, the complexities of desire, or the weight of destiny. Let these themes bubble beneath the plot, giving depth to the characters' dilemmas and substance to the decisions they make. Even your setting can leave a thematic imprint, perhaps with a forest that symbolizes the entanglement of love or a cityscape that reflects the layers of a secret society. Build a story rich in thematic nuance, and readers will carry away more than a tale—they'll take with them a piece of insight that leads to introspection and discussion.

Your aim should be for readers to recall the journey they've shared with your characters long after they finish reading. They should remember the rasping whisper of a ghost's secret, the heat of a lover's gaze, the sting of betrayal, and the sweetness of reunification. Your narrative should be a fabric woven with the fine threads of minutiae that, in their sum, feel like a second skin to your readers—a skin they're reluctant to shed. Craft your prose to leave an indelible mark, so that in idle moments, a reader finds themselves reaching for the comfort of your characters and the world you've created together.

The impressions readers take from your book can be shaped by the emotional arcs of your characters. Illustrate the transformative power of love within the paranormal—how it can heal, shatter, empower, and redeem. Let readers remember your characters not only for their supernatural ties but for the human experiences that love escalates—be it sacrifice, forgiveness, or revelation. These emotions, coupled with the unique experiences of the paranormal, create a tapestry that feels meaningful and memorable. The lasting impact comes from the fusion of the extraordinary with the relatable, delivering an other-worldly story steeped in the human condition.

Consider what elements of your narrative could spark a lasting conversation amongst your readers. Maybe it's the moral ambiguity of a vampire's curse, the societal reflections within a werewolf pack, or the implications of magic in a contemporary setting. Pose questions through your story that don't end with the last page but continue to germinate in the imagination. Let your novel be the beginning of debates, of dreams, of deep-dives into lore and legend. The enduring stories are those that serve as a catalyst for curiosity, that leave readers hungry for more and searching for answers even beyond the confines of the narrative.

When thinking about the impact your story leaves, don't underestimate the power of your setting. A world well-crafted is a destination readers will yearn to return to. Let the mystique of your vampire's castle, the allure of a haunted Victorian London, or the otherworldly beauty of an enchanted forest take root in the readers' minds. Your setting should be as rich and vibrant as any character, leaving an imprint that readers can close their eyes and step into again and again in their daydreams. It's the scent of your enchanted woodland, the echo of footsteps in your ancient halls, that will remain as haunting afterthoughts.

Dialogue can be key in establishing strong reader take-aways. When your characters converse, let their words be layered with meaning, let them display wit, wisdom, and the sparkling charm that will echo in the readers' ears. Every confession of love, every heated argument, every tender consolation should ring with authenticity and emotion. Well-crafted dialogue becomes memorable quotes that readers will whisper to themselves, write down, and share. Through the veracity and vibrancy of spoken words, your characters come alive, stepping off the page to reside in the thoughts and conversations of your readers.

Invite readers to contemplate the 'what ifs' of your story. Present them with a romance and a world that spark extrapolation—what if the protagonists had made a different choice, what if the curse hadn't been broken, what if love hadn't conquered? Let the open-ended possibilities haunt them, the potential alternate realities that lie just a choice away. A narrative that readers can ruminate on, that encourages them to imagine beyond its conclusion, is one that stays with them, lingering in discussions and in their daydreaming reveries.

Engage your readers' empathy by crafting deeply relatable characters facing supernatural obstacles. They should remember how your characters' struggles made them feel, whether it's a werewolf suffering from the duality of their nature or a witch grappling with the ethics of their power. These struggles, although set within a paranormal context, should reflect universal challenges—identity, morality, purpose. When your readers close the book, it's the emotional journey, the trials and triumphs they empathized with, that will leave a lasting impression, resonating amid the echoes of their lives.

The reader takeaways that truly endure are those tied to emotions experienced during pivotal moments in your narrative. Interweave scenes that stir the heart—moments of pure love, utter despair, or triumph. Let these scenes stand out as peaks in the emotional landscape, landmarks of evocation that mark the memory. Craft each pinnacle with care, imbuing them with a raw emotionality that captures the essence of your story. It's these highlighted moments that remain etched in the reader's mind, the snapshots of a story that felt as real as their emotions.

Consider the sensory details in your descriptions—they should leave a lasting sensory impact as if your readers can still smell the roses of an enchanted garden or feel the texture of a forgotten grimoire. Vivid descriptions engrain themselves in the imagination, elements that readers recall with a wistful clarity. Infuse your scenes with specifics that can be recalled easily—flashing eyes, an infectious laugh, the chilling whisper of the wind—all creating a pallet of remembrance. These details anchor the supernatural in the tangible, grounding your ethereal romance in a physical reality easily conjured in the mind's eye.

To leave a lasting impact, the growth of your characters should inspire. Readers often look to characters for strength, and their evolution can motivate personal reflection and self-discovery. As your characters learn to wield their powers or navigate their romance, so too do your readers absorb lessons of perseverance, bravery, and vulnerability. The narrative may conclude, but the growth witnessed can stimulate growth within the reader, an enduring takeaway more precious than the most intriguing plot twist or passionate love affair.

The resonance of a powerful narrative is not confined to one sense alone—through your prose, let the readers not only visualise but feel your story's texture. There's an allure in the rhythm of a ghost's lullaby, the roughness of a hunter's grip, or the silken weave of a spell that impacts across multiple senses. It's the sensory immersion that leaves a multisensory takeaway, giving life to memories that are experienced rather than simply recalled. When a closed book still echoes with the sounds and touches of its world, its impact is profound and lasting.

In the end, you want your readers to remember the experience of reading your book as one might recall a lived romance or a brush with the supernatural—an encounter that was thrilling, moving, and remains unforgettable. It's about crafting a narrative that feels less like a story and more like an encounter with another dimension, a romantic dance with the unknown. Your novel should linger like the memory of a first kiss under a full moon, extraordinary and achingly real in its beauty. When your readers reluctantly part with your characters, they should do so with the anticipation of a reunion, for in their memories, the story lives on.